MISSION OF MERCY

(Branyrd the Angel Series Book 2)

J.E. SPINA

PUBLISHED BY J.E. SPINA

COPYRIGHT 2023
J.E. Spina
Londonderry, New Hampshire

COVER BY JOHN SPINA

ALL RIGHTS RESERVED

ISBN (paperback) 978-1-7361673-9-7

LCCN 2023902737

Thank you for respecting the hard work of this author.

This book is a work of fiction. Any references to persons, places or things are purely coincidental. Names, characters, places, and events are products of this author's imagination.

ACKNOWLEDGEMENTS

A very special thank you to my incomparable beta readers, Patricia Bradley, Michelle Clement James, Michele Rolfe, John Spina and Frances Stewart for working tirelessly to read and review my work and for their helpful input. Their assistance is invaluable and appreciated.

Thank you to my husband, John, for the beautiful cover and for all the dinners he cooked that made it possible for me to continue to write.

DEDICATION

This paranormal fiction is dedicated to my dad who was a proud Marine and would have approved of this story involving Marines.

To all who believe in Angels around us

I think at the conclusion of this book those unbelievers may become believers too.

Table of Contents

PREFACE

This may appear to be a children's book or may be something for middle-graders. But don't let the title or the subject matter confuse you. It is for young adults and 17+.

There are things in this book that cannot be explained to younger children. We all make mistakes but it is how we turn our lives around to correct them that matters. That is what Branyrd must do for not only herself but also for others.

This is the second book in the series. There will be four books, possibly more. Each story will be a stand-alone story dealing in a new mission for the main protagonist. This genre is different from what I have written in the past. I wanted to combine good and evil in a new way through the eyes of an Angel named Branyrd. If you noticed I capitalize the word Angel everywhere in order to make it stand out.

Some may believe in Angels on Earth while others are naysayers. I, for one, believe there is something greater than we are out there that is helping us along our troubled paths and trying to steer us in the right direction. We all need help at one time or another in our lives.

Believe what you may but after reading about this Angel you just may change your mind about believing. I hope this story about Branyrd lightens your hearts, lifts your spirits, and brings a little joy your way.

I wrote this story about a homeless Marine vet in memory of my father who was a proud Marine. He would have cheered Branyrd on.

PROLOGUE

Kylie put down the phone and collapsed into a chair. Tears flowed from her eyes as she grabbed a bottle of wine and drank until she couldn't feel the pain.

She loved her husband and missed him with every fiber of her being. She didn't know what she was going to do. She couldn't think clearly right now. When he went into the Marine Corps, she thought she would die of loneliness, but she found solace in a bottle.

She dragged herself into the bedroom and began to empty her drawers and closet and throw everything that would fit into a suitcase. She couldn't stay here. She had to get away. How would she manage to take care of her son and a husband who was possibly incapacitated mentally. He may not even remember her. Isn't that what the doctor had said on the phone call to inform her of her husband's status. Her husband would have to undergo months or years of therapy.

When they had moved to this small apartment after their son was born, she felt happier than she had ever been in her life. That was until Lucas left on his tour with the Marines.

There was no family on either side to turn to for help. She was lonely and spent time with her neighbor, Ruby, an older spinster woman, who loved Ezra. Her son loved Ruby too. Every time Kylie needed to get out for a drink, she called Ruby to take care of Ezra. Kylie promised herself that she would stop drinking each time.

She looked behind her when she heard her son's voice. "What's wrong, Mommy? Are we going somewhere?"

"Sorry, sweetie. I must go away for a while. I will call Ruby to watch you. Okay? You like Ruby, don't you? She plays games and cards with you."

"Yes, Mommy. But why can't I come with you? Is Daddy coming home soon?"

"Yes...yes, he is, sweetie. He will be home soon and can take care of you."

"Will you come back soon too, Mommy?"

"Umm...yes, soon. I will come back soon."

She hugged and kissed her son as Ruby arrived to take care of him. Kylie pulled herself away from Ezra's tight embrace after a few minutes and said, "Now you be a good boy for Ruby, okay?"

"Yes, Mommy. Please come back soon. I will miss you."

"Okay. Goodbye, sweetie. I love you."

"I love you too, Mommy."

Ruby spoke softly to her, "Kylie, don't do this. Your son needs you, and soon so will your husband. You have to stop drinking. Come back quickly, okay. I will make sure Ezra has dinner and goes to bed. But you must try to stop." Ruby looked at Kylie with a stern expression.

"Thank you, Ruby. I'm doing the best I can," Kylie sighed.

Glancing down at the suitcase that was at Kylie's feet, Ruby inquired, "What is the suitcase for? You can't be thinking of leaving for good, Kylie. What is wrong with you?" Ruby grabbed Kylie's arm to keep her from leaving.

"I have to, Ruby. I need to get away for a couple of days and then I will be back. Thank you for all you have done for me and Ezra. I couldn't have managed without your help." Kylie leaned into Ruby's embrace and hugged her back before Ruby turned to look at Ezra.

Ruby shook her head and sighed, "Please take a day and come back. Ezra needs you, Kylie."

"I promise, I will be back soon, Ruby." Kylie tried to smile. She looked at her son one last time with his curly locks and big brown eyes as he sat waiting for Ruby to play a game. At that moment, Ezra looked up at her and waved.

Kylie sighed heavily and waved back before she opened the door and pulled her suitcase along with her. She leaned heavily on the door once it was closed and closed her eyes and said, *Am I doing the right thing? God help me!*

Once Kylie left the house the tears flowed even more. She got into the waiting taxi and did not look back.

CHAPTER ONE

Branyrd, Angel First Class, was feeling good about how her first mission had gone and was eagerly looking forward to the second.

The only problem with taking on these missions from the LORD was having to leave the humans after she had bonded with them. Her fellow Angels had told her there were some difficult parts of these assignments; they never specified just what though.

She smiled to herself as she visualized the happy faces on the little girl, Annie, and her mother, Maggie, part of her first mission, when she had become their friend. It was such an unbelievable feeling of euphoria to have made these friendships. What was also incredible was having feelings of being more like a human. Branyrd remembered the first time she felt tears on her face and how worried she was about little Annie and her mother. She felt so protective about them. She had never sensed this feeling before. Angels don't worry about anything unless it is something the LORD has tasked them to do.

Angels don't cry or have the emotions as humans do. They interact differently and don't have the issues or problems humans have. Thank God for that!

It was devastating to leave these two beautiful humans but the LORD let Branyrd glimpse them after she left Earth. It was mostly to reassure her that the humans were doing well without her being there. This thought saddened Branyrd when Maggie and Annie no longer needed her.

The LORD assured her she had done an exemplary job on her first mission and not to worry about Annie and Maggie for they were doing well. Besides, HE would be watching over them now.

Branyrd had giggled when the LORD said that, as if HE needed her to watch over them anymore. What was she but an Angel First Class, still not at the top of the classes. She would never be a Guardian Angel like Benedicto who guided her on the first mission, or Archangels like Michael, Gabriel, Raphael and Uriel. They were the chosen ones.

She had to be satisfied with what she was and try to do her utmost best to please HIM. HE had been most forgiving of her setbacks and faults, such as, foul language that came and went unexpectedly. It was as if she couldn't control what came out of her mouth.

When Branyrd was just a cloud at the lower levels of Angels, she spoke through her many orifices in her cloud base. Now that she had a body like a human, she used her mouth to speak. Hopefully, she wouldn't swear again.

Because HE knew all and saw all, she couldn't even think about swearing. HE could zap her with HIS lightning eyes in warning. That was something she did not ever want to see or feel.

As for having a human body, she needed to have one now that she was going on missions to Earth for the LORD. She had to blend into her surroundings and not appear different. This was a difficult thing for her. She was not a human, but on the outside, she looked like one now. She was small in stature in her human body with long blonde hair and hazel eyes that changed color with her moods. She would remain in this form until she returned to Heaven when once again, she would be tall and stately with her Angel wings that shimmered and fluttered as they surrounded her in a protective way.

There were some strange things that humans do that Angels never do. One of these things was to eat and thereafter relieve oneself in rooms called bathrooms. On her first mission she had to make believe she used them. She flushed the toilet and ran the water several times a day. She only hoped she wouldn't have to do any of that again.

She didn't eat food either, just ice cream, chocolate and coffee the last time she was on Earth. Those were her chosen foods and had become her favorites. She had to fake eating everything else and make excuses she wasn't hungry when humans asked why she wasn't partaking. She became skilled at fooling everyone she met. At least, she hoped she did.

Branyrd closed her eyes to go back to Earth and try to imagine how Annie and Maggie were doing now with Nate, the errant husband and father. It looked like Nate had changed his ways from her last glimpse of them moving into their apartment again. They looked happy to be together.

Well, it was time to move on from that mission, for soon she would have another. Branyrd flew over to see her fellow Angels: Lortilla, Angel 3rd Class, Asha, Angel 2nd Class, Adelle, Angel 1st Class, Zemira, meaning song, Angel 1st Class, and Matias, meaning gift of God, Angel 1st Class. They had many questions for Branyrd which she knew she could not answer and she smiled at them saying, "It was the most wonderful experience being on Earth and helping others in HIS name as you know, or at least most of you 1st Class Angels know what I mean. I wish I could share the feelings I had while I was there. But, alas, you understand." All the Angels nodded and smiled back at her, at least the ones with bodies while the clouds just swayed up and down.

Branyrd sighed and thought back to her first mission as she flitted from cloud to cloud. She was startled out of her reverie when she heard a familiar voice calling her name.

"Branyrd, wake up. It's time to get ready to leave."

"Oh, Benedicto! Nice to see you again. You haven't been around lately. I've missed you!"

"Well, I had some other charges to take care of on Earth. You are not my only charge, Branyrd, but you are my favorite! Just don't tell anyone I said that though," he chuckled as he waved his hands over Branyrd.

"That's nice to hear. My lips are sealed! What did you say, Benedicto? It's time?" She felt herself floating downward at a fast pace, one of which she was not comfortable. She opened her eyes to see a familiar place – Earth.

CHAPTER TWO

Branyrd didn't think she would ever get sick of seeing Earth. It had a different kind of beauty than Heaven. It was colorful while Heaven was all white with different shades of blue, dazzling to the eye and almost too bright but in a calming way.

Earth was nothing like she had ever seen before. The sky today was brilliant with shades of blue and pink as she traveled down through the clouds.

She especially loved the changing seasons on Earth. The last time she came, it was in the spring and summer but now it was the end of fall and all the trees were changing colors and dropping their leaves as if in a kaleidoscope. She wanted to touch each leaf to feel it and breathe it all in.

As they got closer, the air felt crisp and clean with scents of pinecones, nuts and leaves. She loved every minute of being here. It was exciting to think about what she would do next and who she would meet. Branyrd only prayed she would meet some nice people again like before. She didn't particularly enjoy meeting the unpleasant ones. But that was how Earth was. There were all kinds of people there in different walks of life and with varied types of personalities and faults.

If anyone knew what it was like to have faults, Branyrd did. She had to make amends all the time for her unacceptable language. She came out of her reveries as her feet hit the ground with Benedicto at her side.

She looked up at him and smiled. "Where to now, Benedicto, my Guardian Angel, First Class Angel on High?"

"No need to use my whole moniker, Branyrd. I am Benedicto to you," he responded with a wink.

"Okie dokie, Benedicto. Lead the way. Where are we?" Branyrd smirked back at him.

"This is Archer, New Hampshire, Branyrd."

As they walked down a dusty sidewalk, Branyrd noticed lots of paper, garbage and articles of clothing strewn about. Along the abandoned storefronts were tents in all sorts of sizes made up of different kinds of material and newspaper while some were just cardboard. There was a odd, unpleasant smell that hung over the area.

Branyrd turned to Benedicto with a questioning brow, "Okay. But what's all this?"

Benedicto turned his face toward Branyrd's and responded in a soft and melancholy tone, "This is where the homeless live."

"Homeless? Holy shit! Oops, sorry LORD! I thought everyone had a home of some kind."

"Well, yes, they do. This is the homeless people's kind of home."

Branyrd gasped in shock, "What? They live in paper tents and on the street? That's not right!"

"Yes, sadly to say, it isn't, Branyrd. But this is the way on Earth," Benedicto said with a sad sigh and a shake of his head.

"But don't they have family to take care of them?"

"Some do and some don't. All of this you will find out soon enough, little Angel."

"I don't understand, Benedicto. If they have family, why aren't they living with them? How do they survive when it gets cold or when it...what's the word?"

"Snows?"

"Yes, snows."

"Some do not make it, unfortunately."

"What? The LORD lets some of them die? How could he do that? That's not right!" Branyrd exclaimed as her eyes filled with moisture at the thought.

"You must understand, Branyrd. The LORD let's everyone decide what they want to do in life. HE will only intercede if they request HIS help. That is why you are here now."

"Do you mean someone asked for help?"

"Yes."

"Is that all you are going to tell me, Benedicto? For… Pete's sake!" Branyrd held her head in her hands as she felt all the pain, suffering and needs of those in this homeless community. She was having trouble dealing with all these feelings being a truly empathic entity.

"Good word choice, Branyrd!" Benedicto guffawed, but quieted down when he saw the distress in Branyrd's face.

"Um, yes. I did have something else in mind though to say to you!"

"I can imagine you did, little Angel," Benedicto responded with a smile filled with amusement. He added with concern, "Are you all right, Angel?"

"Yes, I'm fine, Benedicto. Now are you going to tell me what my mission is?"

"Not yet. Soon, Branyrd, soon."

As Branyrd was sulking over not getting more information from her Guardian Angel, a man came up to her and tapped her on the shoulder.

She turned abruptly and nearly knocked over the slovenly-looking man with a distinct odor about him that was anything but pleasant. She rubbed her nose to get rid of the smell.

"Oh, so sorry, sir. You startled me. What can I do for you? Do you need some help?"

Branyrd looked at Benedicto and nodded in a whisper, "Is this the one I will be helping?"

Benedicto shrugged his shoulders and looked away.

The man waited for Branyrd to turn toward him again before responding, "Are you my sister?"

"No, sorry, I'm not. Are you hungry, sir?"

The man didn't answer and wandered away in a wavering gait.

"What's wrong with that man? Is he drunk or something, Benedicto?"

"I don't know, Branyrd. He just looks tired and lost to me."

"Well, if he isn't the one I need to help, who is?" Branyrd bristled with impatience.

"Calm yourself, Angel. You will know soon enough. You need to watch and observe those around you and then you will know what is expected of you."

"What does that mean, Benedicto? Oh, sometimes you can be so exasperating!" Branyrd sighed and tried to calm down.

Branyrd started thinking, "I didn't feel this way in Heaven. Why do I suddenly feel so wired up and nervous? It must be something to do with the people around me and their feelings. I am absorbing their anguish and despondency through my empathic nature." She closed her eyes and prayed to the LORD for guidance.

When she opened her eyes, what she saw was heartbreaking.

CHAPTER THREE

Standing in front of Branyrd was a little boy about four years old. He had on a tattered pair of pants, shirt and a jacket that was much too big for his small body. He wore a cap with Marines – Semper Fi on it. His face and hands hadn't seen a washcloth in a long time.

He looked up at Branyrd with big brown eyes that had seen a lot of sorrow in a short time. He spoke in a little voice edged with a hoarseness that startled Branyrd.

"Hi. Are you here to help my daddy?"

"Why? Is your daddy sick?"

"Yes, he is very, very sick. He can't get up anymore. I tried to help him."

The little boy raced away from Branyrd before she could ask him where his father was. She followed close behind and called out to Benedicto to come along too but he wasn't there as usual.

The boy went down an alleyway and stopped in front of a trash can. There sitting up against the trash can was a man. His eyes were closed and his face was pale with sunken cheeks and dark circles under his eyes. He moaned as the boy touched his father's arm.

"Daddy, help is here. I told you if I prayed hard enough someone would come to save you," the little boy cried as he hugged his father.

Branyrd knelt to look at the man more closely. "Are you all right, sir? Can you open your eyes?"

The man moaned again but didn't move. The little boy shook his father's arm and tried to wake him so he could respond to the lady.

Branyrd looked at the little boy and asked, "What is your name, little one?"

"I'm Ezra. My daddy's name is Lucas."

"Hello, Ezra. It's nice to meet you. When was the last time you and your father had something to eat?"

"I don't remember. Are you an Angel? You are beautiful! You must be an Angel with your golden hair." Ezra was in awe of Branyrd as he watched her hair sparkle in the light that suddenly appeared behind her.

Branyrd smiled and said, "Do you believe in Angels, Ezra?"

"Yes, I do because I prayed for one to come and help my daddy and here you are."

Branyrd patted Ezra on the head and led him aside to Benedicto who stood behind her with a plate full of food for the child.

Ezra's eyes opened wide at the food and moved closer to take some.

Benedicto washed the boy's hands and face with a cloth he pulled out of his pocket before Ezra could begin eating.

The Guardian Angel produced a chair and a small table to make the boy comfortable while he ate. Ezra was so busy filling his mouth that he didn't notice he was now sitting in a chair with a table in front of him.

Branyrd leaned over Lucas and began to pray. She touched Lucas's face and eyes as the LORD instructed her and waited. Within a few moments Lucas sat up straighter and looked at her in alarm.

"Who are you? Where is my son?" Lucas tried to get up to look for Ezra.

Branyrd waved her hands over Lucas's head to calm him and answered, "I'm sorry to startle you. I'm Branyrd. I am here to help you. Don't worry about Ezra, my um... friend, Benedicto, is taking care of your son. He is right over there having something to eat. Are you hungry, Lucas?"

"I don't understand. Where did you come from and how did you know I needed help?"

Branyrd smiled and said, "Ezra prayed and asked for help for you."

"He what?" Lucas asked in a choked voice.

"He prayed for help. Do you believe in Angels, Lucas?"

"Umm… I don't understand. What are you saying? Are you supposed to be an Angel?"

"I am here to help you and Ezra, Lucas. What can I do for you? Are you sick?"

"I don't know. I sat down and now I can't seem to move. Ezra has been helping me but he is only a little boy. I should be taking care of him, not the other way around."

"I understand, Lucas. Let's get you up and walking. First put your arm around my neck and I will pull you up. You need to eat something to get back your strength."

Branyrd led Lucas over to the table where Ezra was eating. Benedicto produced another chair and helped Lucas sit down after he washed the man's dirty face and hands like he did for Ezra.

Lucas looked around and shook his head. "I must be dreaming. What is happening here? Where did all this food come from?"

"Look, Daddy, there's chicken wings, hot dogs and hamburgers, all my favorite things. This man said that I can have anything I want. All I have to do is ask for it and he will get it for me."

Lucas looked down at his plate that was now filled with his favorite things, steak, baked potatoes, onion rings, and beans. He kept shaking his head as he ate as fast as he could swallow in fear that it may all disappear.

"I don't understand any of this, but I thank you both however you did this. I don't know how to repay you kind people."

"You don't have to repay us, Lucas. You need to get better, stronger so you can take care of Ezra on your own. Do you have a place to stay? Do you sleep in a tent?" Branyrd asked.

"No, I had a box that we used but it was stolen when I fell asleep one day. Now we sleep in the alley next to the trash cans. It's not the best place to be but I plan to find work and then get a room for us."

"I see," Branyrd said as she exchanged concerned expressions with Benedicto.

Benedicto shook his head at Branyrd when she sent thoughts into his head and responded back to her, "No, he cannot come with us. We have to let him stay here. He must work this out himself."

"How is he going to work this out? He doesn't have any money or a place to stay. Why can't we get him a room?"

"That is not what HE wants us to do."

"What does HE want us to do then?" Branyrd asked in exasperation. "Why am I here if I can't help him that way?"

"You will see soon enough. Now we must leave them."

"No, I can't leave them like this," Branyrd cried out in alarm. "They need my help and I am going to give it to them."

Benedicto whisked the table away along with the food once Lucas and Ezra were finished. He waved his hands over their heads to erase everything that had taken place and pulled Branyrd along as he flew them out of the alley and onto another street far from them.

"Why did you do that, Benedicto! I can't believe you did that? What are they supposed to do now? Won't they remember me? At least let them remember me, please!"

"Okay, Angel. Listen, Lucas had plenty to eat and will be strong enough to find work and a place to stay on his own. That is all we can do right now."

"Oh shit, I mean goodness sakes!" Branyrd stated in frustration. "What if they need more help?"

"Then we will see what HE wants us to do. If you noticed, there were many more in need of assistance on the street. Some may not make it through the night. We need to go back and see what we can do to help the others."

Branyrd sat on the curb and held her head in her hands as she tried to keep tears from falling. "It's not fair that these people have to live like this. I can feel their pain and suffering."

"I know, Branyrd. But some of them don't want to live another way. They have made their choices and this is how they want to live."

"What? Why would someone want to live on the street and starve? They never get to use a bathroom, wash up or eat like everyone else."

"I agree, Branyrd. I don't understand it all either. HE said some people don't want to work or deal with everyday problems. They may have mental issues that won't allow them to handle what others can."

"Can I ask HIM for guidance in this case, Benedicto? I need clarification. I want to do the right thing."

"Well, that is up to you and HIM. I won't stand in your way, Branyrd." Benedicto disappeared into thin air after his last word.

"Oh, for …goodness' sake, Benedicto. Why do you keep doing that – disappearing into thin air?"

Branyrd looked up to Heaven and prayed for answers to all her questions. She waited for HIM to tell her what she should do. She knew what she wanted to do but couldn't go against HIS wishes. She knew that HE could whisk her back to Heaven in a second if she tried to do something on her own without HIS approval.

She sighed heavily and waited, but not as patiently as an Angel should.

CHAPTER FOUR

Lucas held onto Ezra's hand as he guided him in and out of stores that were still open. There were no openings for him to work. He would have to walk further away from this decrepit neighborhood where there were more stores to visit. He only hoped that they would not be turned away by their appearances. At least they had clean faces and hands. He couldn't remember washing Ezra's or his own in a long time.

For the first time, in he didn't know how long, his stomach was full. When did he eat? Ezra said he felt full too and didn't remember eating either. Whatever caused this to happen he was grateful.

Ezra asked, "Daddy, where are we going?"

Lucas looked down on his son. "I need to find a job so I can make some money to take care of you, Ezra. Don't you want to have a nice place to sleep, use a bathroom instead of the alley and eat three meals a day?"

"Yes, Daddy. But what if you can't get a job? Will we sleep in the alley again and eat what we can find in the trash?"

Lucas shuddered to think that is how they had been living since he lost his job after coming back from the service and his wife had walked out on them.

"Will Mommy come back and live with us, Daddy?"

"I...I don't know, Ezra. She had to go away. But don't worry I will be here for you always. I will take care of you." Lucas tried to keep the tears from escaping as he hugged his precious little boy.

"I can pray again, Daddy. Maybe someone will hear me in Heaven and send help for us. I don't know what happened to the Angel who was here before."

"I don't know, Ezra. Maybe they will send another one, little man. Don't worry about that now. Let's see what I can find in the next town. Do you feel tired? Can you walk some more?"

"I'm feeling really good, Daddy. I think I can walk a thousand miles."

"Okay, Ezra. Let's keep going," Lucas chuckled over his son's words. He would never give up until he could give his son a good life no matter what. Maybe he should start praying too. It couldn't hurt.

As they continued walking in silence, Lucas's mind wandered back to when he was in the service. He shivered even though he wasn't cold as the memories continued to assail his mind.

Ezra looked up at his father when he felt this shiver run through his hand from his father's. "What's wrong, Daddy? Are you cold?"

"Huh? What did you say, Ezra?"

"I asked if you were cold, Daddy. I felt you shiver right through my hand."

"Oh, no, I'm not cold. It was only a bad daydream, that's all. It's gone now. No worries, my son." Lucas smiled down at his son and squeezed his hand to reassure him. He didn't want his son to be any part of his horrific memories of the war.

Lucas felt his son poking him as Ezra stopped in front of him. "Daddy, look, there's a store over there. Do you want to see if you can get a job?"

"Hmm, I see it now, Ezra. Thank you for bringing it to my attention. Let's go find out." Lucas guided his son across the street and entered the store.

The lady at the counter looked up when she heard the bell ring upon the door opening. "Hi there. What can I do for you?"

Ezra waved and smiled his best smile for the lady. He spoke before his father could, "Can my daddy get a job here? He needs some money to buy food for us and a place to stay."

The lady was speechless at first, then smiled. "Let me see what we can do. What is your name, sir?"

"I'm so sorry about my son's boldness. I was planning on asking that question myself. He just beat me to it."

Lucas put out his hand and introduced himself, "Hi, my name is Lucas and this is my presumptuous son, Ezra."

"Nice to meet you both, Lucas and Ezra. I'm Amy. I am the manager of Safety First. Why don't you come in the back and fill out an application for employment. Then we will see what we may have for you."

"Thank you, Amy. It's a pleasure to meet you too."

Lucas and Ezra followed Amy into the back room and sat down at a table where Amy put the application form and two sodas.

Before picking up the soda, Ezra asked, "Daddy, can I have this drink?"

"Umm, yes, you can, Ezra but you must first say thank you to the kind lady."

"Thank you, Amy. I like ginger ale." Ezra chugged back a few mouthfuls, almost choking.

"Take it easy, Ezra," Amy exclaimed as she patted his back. "Would you like a cookie?"

"Oh, yes please!" Ezra's eyes widened in delight when Amy handed him two large cookies.

"Thank you so much! I love chocolate chip cookies but haven't had one for a long time."

"Really? That's too bad. I made these cookies and have a whole plate full. You can have as many as you want, Ezra, if your father says it's okay."

"Is it okay, Daddy, if I eat these cookies and more?"

"Two cookies are plenty for now, Ezra. Don't bother the kind lady. Sit quietly and eat your cookies. We will be leaving as soon as I complete this form."

"Yes, Daddy." Ezra sat and took big bites out of his cookies and sighed contentedly with a wide smile at Amy.

A short time later Lucas handed Amy his paperwork and thanked her again, "Thank you, Amy, for your kindness to my son and me. I look forward to hearing back from you soon. I know a lot about hardware and safety equipment if that helps you decide."

"Yes, it does help. How will I reach you, Lucas? You didn't put down a phone number or address."

"I'm sorry. I don't have a phone or address just yet. I am looking for a place for my son and me. I can come back here again in a day or so. Is that okay?"

"Well, I guess so. See you soon. Don't forget to take a few more cookies with you, Ezra."

Amy handed Ezra a bag with half a dozen cookies in it for him later.

"Wow, thank you so much, Amy. You are so nice and pretty. I like your long brown hair too."

"Thank you, Ezra. You are quite handsome and sweet yourself. I look forward to seeing you again soon. Bye."

Ezra kept waving at Amy as he walked across the road, then walked the several blocks and back toward their alleyway for the evening. The time had passed quickly for they had walked a long distance. Lucas was happy to have found a place where he could possibly work. He had to get his life back and provide a home and safe environment for his son.

He came out of his thoughts when he heard his son's voice. "She is real pretty, Daddy. Don't you think so? I like her hair. It looks like Mommy's hair."

"Umm, yes it does a little, Ezra. Now let's see what we can do for supper. I don't want you just to eat cookies. I will look around to see what I can find for us," Lucas sighed knowing that the cookies would probably be better than what he would find for them to eat.

***

Branyrd spoke to the LORD about her new mission. She had begged HIM about some background on the father and son but couldn't believe what she saw once HE did.

HE showed her a scene in the past from Lucas's life. She watched in horror as it played out.

CHAPTER FIVE

The land was a jungle, green and impenetrable. The air was hot and thick with the smell of vegetation. Branyrd was startled when she saw men suddenly appear running through the dense greenery with heavy packs on their backs and rifles slung over their shoulders. HE pointed out to Branyrd, "Watch the lead man."

Gunfire could be heard sporadically as the men ran away from it. Soon after there were more men who were chasing the first group through the vegetation.

"What's going to happen, LORD?"

"Wait and see."

Branyrd concentrated on the scene and gasped as all the men were gunned down except for the lead man who continued to run and find a place to hide as the killers ran past him without detection.

"Is that Lucas, LORD?" Branyrd asked in alarm.

"Yes, it is. He lost his whole battalion that day. He had to hide out and then find his way back to his camp for reinforcements. But when he arrived...you will see. Watch."

"There he is again. He is running toward a camp with tents. Where are all the men? Is he alone?"

"Yes, all the men have been killed or captured by the enemy. He is all alone."

"But what can he do? Who will help him?"

"He took what food and supplies he could from his camp and then moved on. He stayed in the jungle living off bugs, greens and drinking rain water for weeks. He somehow survived and found his way to another encampment where he stayed until he could recuperate from exhaustion, sickness and hunger."

"How did he get back home?" Branyrd tried to keep the tears from falling as she felt his suffering.

"He was finally picked up in a rescue helicopter with a few other men who were injured or sick. He has never gotten over losing all his men."

"I see why he is so despondent. What can I do to help him, LORD?"

"He is trying hard to find a way back. But he still suffers from nightmares and daydreams that torment him. It is called PTSD."

"What is PTSD, LORD?"

"It's Post Traumatic Stress Disorder. This can happen to many who have suffered during war or a tremendous episode of heartache or horror."

"Oh, no! Will he die?"

"No, that is why I sent you down to help him get his life back, Branyrd. Do you think you can take on this mission?"

"Yes, I know I can do it. I will do my best, LORD. But what can I do? I don't know where to start."

"You already started, Branyrd, by feeding both him and his son. That is a start. Now you must stay close to him to help him through his PTSD."

"Okay. But…"

Branyrd looked around and she was standing alone at the end of the same alleyway where she had first spotted her new mission charges. She walked back to where she had last seen Lucas and Ezra.

"Daddy, there's the Angel! Look, she is standing where you were laying down. I think she is looking for you."

Branyrd heard Ezra's little voice and turned around to face him and his father. "Oh, there you are. I was just looking for you."

"Hi Angel. Where did you go? We went to get a job. My daddy is going to work at a store down there." Ezra pointed his finger in the direction they had come a while ago.

"I had something to do, but I'm back." Branyrd said after listening to Ezra explain about the store and a job. "Oh, that's good." Branyrd waited for Lucas to say something.

"Yes, I did apply for a job at a hardware store. I don't know if I will get it though. What are you doing back here?"

"I came back to see if I can help you in any way. Are you hungry? I'm sorry I was gone so long."

Ezra spoke up waving his bag of cookies, "I have chocolate chip cookies from Amy. I ate two already but Daddy says I can't eat cookies for supper. But we don't have anything else to eat."

"Who is Amy?" Branyrd asked curiously.

"She is the nice lady who works in the store we went to."

"Oh, okay. Hmm, well, let's see what I can do. Maybe you would like to have a hamburger and fries and a milkshake."

"Oh yes, yes!! Daddy, do you want a burger, fries, and a milkshake too?"

"Ezra, we can't bother this nice woman with our problems. I will find something for us to eat."

Before Lucas could take Ezra's hand and lead him away, Branyrd had a table set with the burgers, fries, and shakes for them. She waved them over and said, "Please eat your fill. It is my pleasure to help you."

"But...how did you do this?" Lucas asked in confusion.

"Don't worry. Just eat. I will tell you later."

Ezra was already eating with gusto and smearing ketchup and mustard all over his little smiling face. When Lucas saw the joy on his son's face, he sat down next to him and ate. He never took his eyes off the woman who had set this table though. He felt as if he were dreaming – but a good dream not a nightmare for a change.

CHAPTER SIX

Branyrd didn't wait for Benedicto to whisk away the table and food; she did it herself for the first time after getting help from the LORD. She also waved her hands over Lucas and Ezra to erase everything but herself and Benedicto in their minds as the LORD had instructed.

She turned toward Lucas and Ezra as they appeared confused, which was understandable. She filled in the void with conversation to get them to concentrate on her and not on what was missing in their minds. "How do you feel? Are you hungry?"

"Umm, surprisingly not, which I do not understand," Lucas stated with a furrowed brow.

"Me too! I'm stuffed again! What did we eat, Daddy?"

Lucas smiled at his son and shrugged his shoulders. I guess someone must be taking care of us."

"I think it's the Angel, Daddy! See, she did this. She made us full so we wouldn't be hungry. Didn't you, Angel?"

"Did I? You can call me Branyrd, Ezra. Okay?"

"Okay, Branyrd. How did you fill our bellies? Where is the big man who was here before?" Ezra asked as he looked closely at the Angel's green eyes that were sparkling like stars.

"I don't know. How would I do that, Ezra? Do you think I can do magic? The big man's name is Benedicto. He will be by later."

"Yes, I think you can do magic if you are an Angel! Angels live in Heaven, right?" Ezra scrunched up his nose in an adorable way as Branyrd tried not to laugh at this sweet expression.

"Well, yes, Angels do live in Heaven, Ezra. But I don't think we can do magic. We can only do what the LORD asks or allows us to do in HIS name."

"Hmm, I don't understand, Branyrd. What does that mean?"

Branyrd reached for Ezra's hand and held it between hers. "Let me try to explain it to you. The LORD watches over all of us and we must always do as HE says. If HE wants me to come here to help you, HE can give me powers in order to do that."

"So, you do have powers, Branyrd?" Ezra's eyes widened in surprise. Turning to his father he exclaimed, "I knew it, Daddy. Branyrd is a magical Angel! She is the one who made us full so we wouldn't be hungry too much."

Branyrd smiled and shrugged her shoulders. "It's all because of your prayers, Ezra. Didn't you pray for someone to help your daddy?"

"Yes, I did and you came. I am so happy you came, Branyrd. Are you our very own Angel? Are you here to help only us?"

"Well, so far, I am. But HE may want me to help others while I am here also. There are many homeless who need help all around this area."

"I know. Someone took our cardboard box to sleep in. Now we have nowhere to sleep. It gets cold at night." Ezra did a little shiver for Branyrd.

"Hmm, yes, I see it does. It feels like the temperature is dropping now. Would you like me to get you a blanket, Ezra?"

"Oh, yes, please. One for Daddy too!"

"You must first close your eyes and when you open them you will have a place to sleep."

"Okay." Ezra said as he put his hands over his eyes and told his daddy to do the same.

"Can I look yet, Branyrd?" Ezra chattered as he jumped up and down in anticipation.

Branyrd had arranged an extra-large box with a bed, pillows and blanket. She placed some clean clothes for both father and son on the bed. She also put a flashlight inside for light and a book for Ezra to read, along with his cookies on a little table.

"Okay, you can open your eyes, Ezra, you too, Lucas."

Branyrd stood next to the box bedroom as a scream of delight was heard from Ezra and a surprised gasp from his father as they took in the sight of their box bedroom.

"I love it, Branyrd! How did you do that? It must be magic, Daddy. Isn't it?" Ezra pulled his father inside the box and lay down on the bed with a big sigh. He saw the clothes on the bed and spotted the flashlight and the book at the same time and exclaimed, "Look, I have new clothes, a book and a flashlight so I can read it! Will you read it to me, Daddy? What does it say?"

Lucas picked up the book and read, "*Make Believe: Bedtime Stories for Children.*"

"You can read it every night for me, Daddy! Right at bedtime. Can you read it now even though I'm not ready to go to sleep yet."

"Of course. But first we must thank Branyrd for giving us this amazing bed and your book."

"I was going to do that, Daddy! I was just too ex... about my bed and book to remember. Sorry."

Lucas laughed, "You mean excited, Ezra?"

"Yes, excited. That's how I feel!" Ezra giggled.

Poking his head out of the box he said, "Thank you, Branyrd! I love the clothes, bed, book and flashlight. This is my first book and flashlight! I can't wait for Daddy to read the book to me. Can I keep it to read every night?"

"Of course, it is my gift to you, Ezra. I hope you enjoy it!"

"I know I will. It has animal stories in it. I saw the animals on the cover. They are cool!"

"I have to leave now, Ezra. The LORD is calling me. Good night, sleep well."

"Will I see you tomorrow, Branyrd?"

"Yes, I hope so. If HE wants me to."

"Okay. I hope HE does. Good night, Branyrd."

Ezra went back inside, changed into his new clothes, lay on his soft, warm bed and opened his book.

"I need to speak with Branyrd, Ezra. You look at your book. I'll be right back."

"Okay, Daddy."

"Excuse me, Branyrd. Don't leave yet. I want to thank you for everything. I don't know how we will ever repay you for this bed, clothes, food and for making my son so happy. I've tried to do my best but…"

"I know. You have had a difficult time, Lucas. I will be back to help you in any way I can. You need to get back on your feet again and then everything will work out."

"I hope so. Only….my wife…some things may not work out."

"I understand. When you are ready, I am here to listen."

"I appreciate that. But not yet. I hope to work that out on my own, for my son's sake."

"Lucas, about the box, it will disappear once you are both out of it. Make sure Ezra takes his book and flashlight with him when he gets outside and his cookies too."

"Oh, I…don't understand how. But I will make sure he does. Thank you again, Branyrd. You really are an Angel sent from…somewhere."

"Somewhere," Branyrd said and smiled.

Lucas ducked his head to get inside but not before turning to see Branyrd one more time. However, she was gone.

CHAPTER SEVEN

Benedicto was walking among the tents and spreading his hands over all inhabitants sleeping there. He turned to look at Branyrd when she bumped into his side to get his attention.

"What are you doing, Benedicto?"

"I am spreading the LORD's love over all as HE requested. HE wanted to give these men, women and children a good night's sleep for a change. HIS love will keep them warm."

"Hmm, that's a good idea. I made my two missions a box bedroom to keep them warm and safe. HE told me I should use my ingenuity along with HIS help. I couldn't have done that without HIM."

Benedicto opened a space in front of his face to look at the box bedroom as if looking through a window. Branyrd peered around the Guardian Angel's shoulder to see how Lucas and Ezra were doing in their box. She smiled and sighed, "See, they are snug, warm and comfortable. Most of all they are safe from danger. No one will be able to see them or the box while they are inside."

"Clever work for a newbie Angel!" Benedicto snickered.

"Thank you, Benedicto! I am honored by your words. I am learning, slowly but surely, I guess. Sometimes it is a miracle I can do anything right."

"I wouldn't say that, Branyrd. I think…well it doesn't matter what I think, but it does matter what HE thinks."

"I know but I value your feedback too, Benedicto." Branyrd put her hand on the Guardian Angel's arm to get his attention.

"Well, I'm happy to say that you are doing a fabulous job, little Angel! I am honored to be along with you on this mission of mercy. You certainly have come a long way. Your language has improved big time too."

"Damn right! Oops! Sorry about that! I got too excited with your compliments and forgot myself. I guess you could call it a mission of mercy. These homeless people are at our mercy for help."

"So, I see, Angel, you do sound excited." Benedicto turned away so Branyrd wouldn't see his amused expression.

An echoey titter could be heard high above them that reverberated all around and then disappeared.

"What was that, Benedicto?" Branyrd asked in alarm.

"Oh, I think you already know, little Angel."

Branyrd kept her eyes Heavenward and looked all around her just in case HE was there.

Benedicto pulled Branyrd out of her reverie. "Listen, Angel. We have much work to do. We need to turn one of these vacant buildings into a place for these homeless to stay out of the cold. We also must get them some portable bathrooms. The weather is turning much colder and there may possibly be some snow."

"Snow? I've never seen snow before. I can't wait to see it and feel it. It's really cold, right? You said portable bathrooms?"

"Yes, to both questions. First, they need to stop relieving themselves on the street. Second, snow is quite cold and wet. If these people stay out in it, they will surely…"

"No! No one is going to die on my watch, Benedicto. Let's get going. What do we need to do?"

"City Hall is our first stop. We need to convince someone that a shelter is needed here and right away for these poor people."

"Okay. What do we say to convince whoever is in charge there?"

Branyrd followed the Guardian Angel to City Hall. She rode an elevator for the first time. She pressed too many buttons before Benedicto could stop her and they had to stop at each floor. A few others riding with them were not happy. All Branyrd could do was smile at them and look innocent.

They arrived at their floor and were directed to the mayor's office. The secretary looked up as they walked in.

"Can I help you?"

"Umm. Yes. I would like to speak to the mayor or whoever is in charge."

"Do you have an appointment?"

"No, but it's of utmost importance about the homeless population in the city. I just left them. I'm worried some will die in the storm that is coming this way."

Branyrd turned to ask Benedicto for help but he was nowhere in sight again. She mumbled to herself, *where are you, Benedicto, when I need you?*

"I understand. Mayor Cramston is quite busy right now. He has meetings tonight. I'm sorry. You will have to make an appointment for another time."

"But, what about the homeless? They may die overnight. It can't wait. You must fit me in right away. I will wait right here." Branyrd sat down and stared at the secretary until the woman felt compelled to pick up her phone and call the mayor.

A few minutes later a large, overweight and sweaty man, his jacket bulging with buttons ready to pop, thinning hair and a broad smile came out of his office to greet Branyrd.

"Well, hello. I'm Mayor Cramston. Who may you be, young lady?" He reached his fleshy hand out to Branyrd waiting for her to introduce herself.

"Nice to meet you, Mayor Cramston. I am Branyrd from Haven. I am only here on a short visit."

"My pleasure to meet you too, Branyrd. Haven, you say? Must be in Massachusetts? What can I do for you, Branyrd."

The mayor took Branyrd by the elbow and guided her into his office. "Please make yourself comfortable, Branyrd, and tell me what has you all upset. My secretary said you were quite compelling and adamant about the homeless."

"Yes, I am adamant about the homeless. There is a snowstorm coming to this area overnight and I fear it will harm many of those sleeping out in the elements. We have to do something to help them."

Mayor Cramston put his hand on his chin and said, "Hmm, I see. I didn't realize there was a storm coming tonight. There was no mention of it on the TV a short while ago."

"Well, I have a friend who knows these things beforehand. He told me that it is a bad one coming this way."

"Okay. Well, let me say this. I have done all I can to help those sleeping on the streets for years. They ignore my efforts. They keep coming back and more and more are here year and after year. I don't know what to do with them. I tried to get them jobs to keep them busy and off the street. We feed them when we can but they never move. This is the life they have chosen. It is not a good life but it's their wish to be left alone."

"I don't understand why they stay this way either if they are given a chance to work and get off the streets. If they won't leave, can we at least open up the empty stores and let them sleep inside on the brutally cold nights?"

"Who is going to fund the heating in those buildings? Who is going to watch over them so that they don't destroy these buildings? The buildings do not belong to the city. They are privately owned and for sale."

"Oh, I see. Can you give me time to come up with a plan to get the homeless off the streets and into the buildings? Can I have a list of who owns those empty stores? I will speak with each owner and see what we can do to help the homeless."

"If that is what you want to do. Go ahead. But I warn you, they will not cooperate unless you buy out each building yourself. We've tried something like this before. It didn't work out. They won't budge. I think they would rather have the stores deteriorate on their own than use them for this purpose. It's a shame."

"I will do my best, Mayor Cramston. Thank you for your time. I will get back to you with my proposal."

"Okay. Let me ask my secretary to get those names and phone numbers of the businesses. I look forward to hearing how you do and what your proposal entails. Good luck, Branyrd. It was a pleasure meeting such an energetic entrepreneur as yourself."

"Thank you, for your help, Mayor."

The secretary gathered the information Branyrd needed and went back to her work. The Angel left with the list in her hand as she pulled open the door to leave. Outside the elevator Benedicto waited.

"Well, how did you do, Angel?" Benedicto said looking smug.

"No thanks to you, Benedicto. I had to make it up as I went along with Mayor Cramston. I had no idea what to say but it came to me with the help of you know who."

Benedicto chuckled, "I knew you would be fine on your own. You really don't need me, Angel. You are very capable of doing everything yourself now. You are on your second mission and no longer a newbie Angel."

"So, you keep telling me, Guardian Angel. I don't feel capable though. This is something way above my Angel grade."

"I disagree, Branyrd. HE put you on this mission for a reason – because you can do anything you put your mind to without my help. I am only here to get you safely here and back to Heaven. That is all."

"Well, it certainly doesn't appear that way to me, Benedicto. You did help me with Lucas and Ezra before."

"I did help a little until I knew you were okay on your own. Look how you handled the box bedroom. That was brilliant thinking, Angel. I don't think I could have done that better myself," he chuckled.

"Enough already, Benedicto. Can we discuss what I want to do about the homeless now?" Branyrd explained what transpired between her and the mayor and how she now had names and phone numbers for the owners of all the buildings.

"What is your next step, Branyrd?" Benedicto observed her in deep thought.

"I'm thinking, Benedicto. I'm thinking. I never had to do such deep reasoning before."

"Yes, I can see smoke rising from your head, Branyrd. You are burning up in thought," Benedicto guffawed.

Branyrd whispered not too nice things as she frowned at her Guardian Angel. *Oh damnit. Sorry, LORD! He exasperates me!*

HE responded, "Calm yourself down, Angel. You have much to do to complete this mission. I am here if you need counseling and so is Benedicto. He is a good sort and only wants the best for you. He likes to razz you, that's all. It's his quirky sense of humor."

"Yes, I can see that," Branyrd sighed and looked around for Benedicto who was no longer there. *No kidding*, she sighed.

She pulled out her list and began the calls from a cell phone that suddenly appeared in her pocket. "Thank you, LORD." Branyrd raised her eyes to Heaven and smiled. "How do I use this?"

HIS voice appeared in her head with directions on how to use this foreign object in her hand. She had never needed one in Heaven.

CHAPTER EIGHT

"Hello."

"Umm, hello. My name is Branyrd. I am interested in your store on Ashley Street."

"What? You want to purchase my store? Is this some kind of a joke?"

"Oh, no sir. I am really interested in it for the homeless who are living outside your store. I want to help…"

The phone call ended abruptly before Branyrd could explain what she wanted to do. She sighed and put a note next to the store and owner's name and went to the next on the list.

After several calls that ended in a similar fashion, she shook her head and raised her eyes to Heaven. *What am I supposed to do, LORD? No one will listen to me.*

"Keep doing what you are doing, Branyrd. Don't give up. You will find what you need soon."

"But..." Branyrd looked at the next name on the list – Poster. She dialed the number and waited.

"Hello, Mr. Poster, my name is Branyrd. I am interested in your store on Ashley Street."

"Really? That is interesting. No one is ever interested in my place. It has been on the market for a couple of years now. Why do you want it?"

Branyrd took a deep breath and began her tale. "I want to help the homeless get off the street there. If I can purchase the vacant stores and transform them into places for the homeless to sleep, eat and gather safely out of the cold, I would save many of them from dying."

"I see. You are one of those."

"What do you mean, one of those?"

"I have received calls like yours before who want me to donate my store for the homeless. Anyway, how will one little store help keep hundreds off the street? What makes you think that they won't go back on the street again after using it to get out of the cold?"

"I don't know that. I agree with you. One store won't be enough. I plan to use all the stores on the block. One part will be for sleeping, another for eating, one for medical care and one for socialization."

"Well, it looks like you have thought this over carefully. How many stores have you acquired so far?"

"None, sir. I was hoping yours would be the first of many. If one owner agrees to my plan then the others will fall in line."

"You think so. What did you say your name was?"

"Branyrd, sir. Yes, I think so. Will you be the first owner to agree?"

"Do you know the price of my store, Branyrd? Are you sure you can afford that?"

"Well, I don't have any money yet but I plan to get some soon. I need your promise that you will think about this and not sell it to anyone else. Okay?"

"I see. You don't have any money but want to buy all these stores on Ashley Street. How do you think you will be able to do that without funds?"

"I have a plan. As soon as it comes to fruition I will call you back, Mr. Poster."

"All right. I will give you a week. If anyone else comes forward to purchase it after that time I will have to renege on this arrangement. Do you understand?"

"Oh, yes. I understand, Mr. Poster. I promise to get back to you before a week's time."

"Well, I guess I will be hearing from you then. Nice talking to you, Branyrd. I wish you luck for both of us. If you can figure out a way to raise the funds, it will take a miracle to do all that you want to do."

"Yes, it may take a miracle, Mr. Poster. It may. Good bye.

***

Branyrd called out to Benedicto, "Where are you Guardian Angel on High? I need your assistance."

"Yes, Branyrd. What is it you need?" he said as he appeared in front of her.

She explained what she had discussed with Mr. Poster and what she wanted to do with the stores on the street. "I know it may take a miracle like Mr. Poster said but I want to try to come up with a plan without using magic as such."

"Hmm, you have piqued my interest, little Angel. What is your plan?"

CHAPTER NINE

Branyrd walked up and down the street checking out all the storefronts which were all attached by squinting into the windows. They looked like they were in good shape without any damage inside. They needed a painting on the outside which she knew she could try to do with some help from Benedicto.

She kicked at the few inches of snow that covered the ground and bent to touch it to make sure it was as cold as Benedicto had told her. She pressed some in her hand and made a ball, squeezing it until it melted. She smiled to herself. She could now say that she had seen and touched snow. She wiped her hands on her jacket and continued to inspect the stores.

Some of the homeless watched her as she paraded up and down looking into the stores. One man came up to her and tapped her on the shoulder. "What are you doing, miss?"

Branyrd jumped back in alarm. "Oh, I didn't hear you behind me. I am checking out the condition of the stores."

"Why are you doing that?" the man asked.

A few others came forward out of curiosity. They all had the best night's sleep and felt the warmest ever despite the cold snap and the few inches of snow that had covered the city.

They listened along with the man as Branyrd answered the man's question about her strange actions. She told them about using the stores for their sleeping, eating and recreation plus medical care too.

One thin and pale-faced older woman coughed before speaking, "Sorry, I don't understand. Why do you want to do this? No one wants to help us. All they want is for us to go away."

"I understand. I don't want you to go away but I do want you to be safe, warm, well-fed and cared for if you don't have any other places to go."

"Oh, well. That's nice of you. But why do you want to do that? What do you get out of it?"

Branyrd smiled and laid a hand on the woman's bony shoulder that was barely covered with a ragged shirt. "I want to help you get back on your feet. It is my mission to help others in HIS name."

"HIS name? What does that mean?"

The crowd around Branyrd was growing as they waited to hear what she would say next.

"Do you believe in the LORD? Do you pray?"

"No, HE wouldn't listen to the likes of any of us," one man said as he tried to raise himself up from a sitting position.

"What is wrong with your legs, sir," Branyrd asked the man who couldn't move."

"I haven't been able to walk in a long time. I don't know why my legs don't work. They just don't. I drag myself around. Sometimes one of my fellow squatters helps me."

Branyrd raised her eyes to Heaven and whispered, "Please help him, LORD."

HE answered back and told her, "Raise your hands over his legs and pray, Branyrd. I will do the rest."

"Yes, LORD," Branyrd said and followed HIS directions.

The man looked up at Branyrd and stated in a shocked voice, "I can feel my legs! They are tingling! I can feel my legs!"

Others crowded around him and raised their voices in surprise as the man began to stand with Branyrd's help as she pulled him up.

"What...what happened? Is this a miracle? I can't believe it? Are you an Angel or something?" the man sputtered as he moved around tentatively.

Branyrd smiled at him and said, "I didn't do anything. It was all HIM. HE cured you, sir. What is your name?"

"I'm Harold. I can't thank you or HIM or whoever did this enough. I…I am truly grateful. I…I…" the man choked as tears flowed soaking his shirt.

Everyone around came out of their tents to see what the commotion was all about. They whispered and pointed to Branyrd and the man now walking on his own.

"Did you see that?"

"She must be an Angel."

"She performed a miracle on Harold."

"He can walk"

"He has never walked since he has been here."

Benedicto appeared at the back of the crowd and smiled at Branyrd. He spoke to her mind, "See, I told you. You can do anything you put your mind to, little Angel."

"It wasn't me. It was HIM. I didn't do anything."

"Oh, I don't know about that. You have more magic in you than you think, Branyrd."

Branyrd watched all the men and women patting Harold on the back as he walked back and forth in front of them all to show off his renewed ability.

Others came over to Branyrd in a long line. "Can you help me too?" one woman asked in a shaky voice. I can't see as well as I used to. Everything is cloudy."

Branyrd raised her hands over the woman's eyes and prayed looking up once again beseeching HIM to help her.

The woman cried out, "I can see! I can see!" She danced around waving her hands up in the air as she twirled and twirled taking in all the people around her. "I can see all of you now! I didn't realize how old and ugly you all are!" she giggled as everyone frowned at her.

Voices were raised in excitement as they crowded around Branyrd and pushed and shoved to get to her next. "Help me! "Help me next!" they cried.

Benedicto came over to Branyrd and pushed the crowd back. He commanded in a strong voice, "Don't push and shove. You will all be taken care of soon enough. You must wait your turn."

Branyrd smiled and spoke in a loud voice, "Listen, everyone. You must go back to your tents. I will come visit each one of you in time. I have much to do right now and will need your help in completing my mission."

"Your mission? What does that mean?" one man asked, who was holding his arm protectively against his chest.

"We all have missions in life to complete. My mission is to help others in need. What is wrong with your arm?" Branyrd asked the man.

"Oh, it's nothing. I'm fine. You must take care of some of the others who are too sick to come out of their tents."

"I will visit each one of you, I promise. But first, let me see your arm. Can you straighten it?"

"No, it has been like this since I came back from the war."

"The war?" Branyrd asked in confusion. "Which war?"

"Oh, I am quite old. It was Vietnam.

"Vietnam? Really? That was a long time ago. How old are you?"

"Too old to say. I don't really know how old I am. But soon I won't have to worry about that any more. I don't' think I will be here much longer."

"What do you mean?" Branyrd asked as she touched his arm.

"I think the LORD wants me to come home. It's time for me."

"Oh no. I don't think HE wants you yet. I think HE may have some other missions for you to tackle first. What is your name, sir? What branch of the service were you in?"

"I'm Fred. Semper fi! I was in the Marine Corps, a proud Marine at that. I served my country and here I am living on the street. I couldn't get a job and now I am too old to care."

"How long have you been living here? Do you have family?"

"I didn't always live here. It's been many years since I traveled from place-to-place living off the street. I settled here a few years ago after my wife died and my children moved away. I don't see them at all. I think they are ashamed of me."

"I'm sorry to hear that, Fred. Once we get things moving here maybe your kids will come and visit you."

Fred grumbled and sighed, "That will be the day!"

Before the man realized, he was using his arm and waving it around as he spoke.

"Look! You are moving your arm, Fred. You can move your arm!" one woman announced.

"Oh, my word! Yes, I can move my arm. What did you do? You must be an Angel. You touched my arm and now it is healed!" Fred reached out to Branyrd and gave her a hug.

"Thank you, thank you! You really are an Angel from Heaven."

"I didn't do that. You know who did that, Fred. It is the LORD. See, HE has a mission for you also to complete before HE brings you home."

"Maybe you are right, Branyrd. What do you think HE wants me to do?"

"We must pray and find out."

"Okay. But it's been a long time since I prayed. How do I do that?"

Branyrd recited the Lord's Prayer for Fred and everyone joined in. She blessed herself and others followed in turn.

She looked out at all the homeless who were gathered in front of her. "I think I know what HE wants us to do. Will you all help me?"

A rousing chorus of 'Yes' could be heard.

"Excellent! This is what we will do. I will need Fred to lead the way for all of us. Can you do that, Fred?"

"Yes! I will do whatever HE wants me to do, Branyrd. It's about time I stood up and did something worthwhile again."

"Great! Perfect!" Branyrd gushed in relief. She now had her own force to move forward with her plan.

Branyrd visited with each homeless person in their tents of newspaper and cardboard. She helped all who needed assistance to get back on their feet. She needed everyone to help complete the tasks she would present to them.

CHAPTER TEN

The next day in the alleyway a short distance away, Ezra and Lucas came out of their tent and it disappeared in a flash. Lucas had told Ezra to keep his book and flashlight and cookies in his hand as directed by Branyrd.

"I ate all the cookies already, Daddy, but I have my book and flashlight, see. Where did our box go? Will it come back so we can sleep there again tonight?"

"I don't know, Ezra. Maybe you can ask Branyrd if she comes back here."

As they were walking down the alleyway to the street Branyrd appeared in front of them.

"You are both looking handsome in your new clothes. How did you sleep last night, Ezra? Lucas?"

Ezra spoke up in an excited voice, "Oh, I slept really good, Branyrd! Thank you so much for these new clothes! They fit just right. I love my book, too. Thank you again. Daddy read it to me last night and again this morning."

"You slept well, Ezra.," his father corrected him.

"That too, Daddy," Ezra responded with a smile.

"That's wonderful to hear, Ezra. I will get you another book if you like."

"Oh, yes, I would love another book!"

"Okay. What about you, Lucas? Did you sleep well?"

"Yes. Thank you for that. It's been a long time since I slept that well."

"Branyrd, where did our box go? Will it come back again for tonight?" Ezra asked as he touched the Angel's hand to get her attention.

"I will see what I can do, Ezra."

"Good! See, Daddy, I told you Branyrd would bring it back again." Ezra was all smiles as he hugged his father.

Lucas tousled his son's curls and said, "That's nice of you, Branyrd. Thank you."

"You are welcome, Lucas. Can I speak to you about something?"

"Sure, anything I can do to repay you for your kindness."

Branyrd explained what she wanted to do with the stores. "Do you think you can assist another Marine who is living on the street?"

"Of course. Do you mean, Fred?"

"Yes. You know him?"

"Oh, all of us know each other. We help each other all the time. We are like a family. No one else wants anything to do with us."

"I'm sorry to hear that, Lucas. Not that you are a family but that no one wants anything to do with you. That's so sad." Branyrd hung her head and sighed.

"What do you want me to do?" Lucas asked, inquisitively.

"Well, I will need help in getting the storefronts painted after I acquire the funds to purchase them. There will also be plenty to do inside setting up the beds, kitchen, medical and social areas, bathrooms, showers and a laundry room."

"Wow, you are going to do all that for us? How are you going to get the funds? There are a lot of stores to purchase."

"Yes, I know. I will need all the help I can get to do it all."

"Maybe I can enlist my buddies to come help. I have some Marines who will do all they can to get this up and running along with us. They have been trying to get me off the street but I have not been receptive. I guess I was giving up. I know that's not a good thing to do, especially with Ezra. I have to get back on my feet for him."

"That would be perfect, Lucas. Let's get all the help we can to see this to fruition."

"Okay. I will have to call my friend and he will get the others on board. Do you think I can get a phone?"

"Of course. In fact, I have one in my pocket at this moment. Here. Do you know his number?"

"I'm not sure. I can look it up online."

"Here you go. Let me know what else you need. I'll be right here with Ezra."

"Can you read me a story, Branyrd, while my daddy is on the phone? I really love the stories about the bear, the dragon and the alien, Blue. They are so cool!"

"Sure, come here, Ezra. Let me get a comfortable chair for us to sit on."

A chair materialized in front of them with puffy cushions, a high back and large rounded and tufted arms.

"Wow, this is so cool, Branyrd. How did you do that? Can you teach me?"

"Sorry, Ezra, I can't. I don't even know how I did it." Branyrd laughed.

Ezra giggled in response and sat next to Branyrd since the chair was wide enough for two and settled back to hear the stories that were becoming his favorite.

Lucas was busy on the phone once he found his friend's number and explained in detail Branyrd's plan.

"Who is this Branyrd you keep mentioning, Lucas?" his fellow Marine, Cam, asked.

"You wouldn't believe it if I told you, Cam. Sorry, I can't share everything but just do what you can to enlist the rest of the guys. We will need all the help we can get to make this possible."

"I'll do my best, Lucas. Say, it's good to hear that you sound positive and upbeat for a change. We have all been worried about you and Ezra."

"Thanks, Cam. Yes, I do feel much better. I may even have a job soon. Things are beginning to look up for me. It's about time, isn't it, buddy?"

"Yes, I would say so, Lucas. I'll get back to you as soon as I have all the guys on board. Can we talk soon? We need to set up a meeting time."

"I will check with Branyrd to see when she will need all of you. Talk to you soon, Cam. Thanks again!"

"My pleasure, Lucas. I can't wait to tell all the guys about this. They will be pleased to see you back to normal or almost there."

Lucas looked over at his son and the Angel snuggled up on a large tufted chair. *Where did that come from? Strange things keep happening here since Branyrd arrived. Maybe I am dreaming.*

"Hi Daddy. Branyrd read all the stories to me while you were on the phone. I love this book. Branyrd said she is going to bring me another book soon."

"That's cool, son! Soon you will be reading it all by yourself."

"Yes, I will. Then I can go to school. I read a little with Branyrd. She taught me a couple of words. She said I should be going to school."

"I know, Ezra. I will register as you soon as I get my job and a place for us to stay. Okay?"

"Okay, Daddy. I can't wait."

Branyrd looked over Ezra's head and met Lucas's eyes. She nodded and smiled at him and Lucas smiled and nodded back.

"How did your phone call go?"

"It was successful. I got in touch with my friend, Cam. He is going to enlist the help of all our fellow Marines. We should have quite a few here whenever you need them."

"That's delightful news, Lucas. Let me see what I can do to find the funds to purchase the places first. I have an idea that might work."

"Really? How are you going to do that?"

"Well, I will be visiting all the stores on the next block for assistance. Would you like to come with me?"

"Sure. I planned to visit the Safety-First Hardware Store to find out if I got the job there. Maybe if I get the job, I can convince the manager to donate something for your mission as you call it, Branyrd."

"Sounds good to me, Lucas. I'm sure you will get the job, don't worry." Branyrd looked up to Heaven and smiled.

CHAPTER ELEVEN

The threesome walked to the Safety-First Hardware Store. Lucas went in while Branyrd stayed with Ezra outside. She wanted to give Lucas some time to talk to the manager. She knew he would get the job. She had put in a good word for him with you know who.

Lucas bounced out of the store as if he were on springs. "I got it! Can you believe it? I got it!" He swung Ezra around in a circle.

"Hurray, Daddy! Now we can get our own place to stay inside and I can have a real bathroom and a bed." Turning to Branyrd he announced, "It's not because I don't like your box bedroom, Branyrd. I just want to have a whole room to myself."

"I understand, Ezra. It's okay. You should have your own place to stay."

"Also, Branyrd, I asked Amy at the store if she would be interested in donating something to your efforts to help the homeless."

"What did she say, Lucas?"

"She said she would leave it up to me to put a box at the register that says, "Help the Homeless.""

"That's a good idea. Nice of her to do this"

"Yes, I told her that too. She is a kind woman. I can see this in her eyes. They are like your eyes, Branyrd. There is depth and kindness there."

"Oh, thank you, Lucas. How sweet of you to say." Branyrd blushed in surprise. It wasn't often she received a compliment such as this.

"I told you, Daddy. I like Amy. She is pretty and has nice hair too like Mommy's. When is Mommy coming home, Daddy? She has been gone for years and years," Ezra sighed and lowered his head.

"It hasn't been that long, Ezra. I'm sure it feels like it to you though. That is my next task, son. We will find Mommy and bring her home, okay? Don't worry about that now. We have much to do to help our friend, Branyrd. Right? I'm sure she has some work for you to do too."

"Umm, why yes, I do, Ezra. I have some special tasks for you to complete. Come with me."

Ezra took Branyrd's hand and Lucas followed close behind. She headed back to the storefronts and pointed out all the ones that would need painting and fixing.

"I can't paint, Branyrd. I am too short to reach everything."

"Oh, I know, Ezra, but there is more to do than just painting. I want you to hold a sign in front of you and show it to anyone who passes by in a car or walking. I want everyone to know what we are doing here."

"Okay. What is the sign going to say, Branyrd?" Ezra asked.

"Let's see. It should say, 'Help the Homeless by your Donations Today.'"

"Do you think that will work, Branyrd?" Lucas asked with uncertainty.

"Let's see what we can do. Let me get the signs and try it out right now."

With a wave of her hand, she pulled up several signs for not only Ezra to hold and wave around but also enough for the other homeless.

The homeless men and women who Branyrd helped in some way or another came forward eagerly to hold the signs and wave them around to anyone who passed by.

There were some surprised looks on the drivers of the cars who passed. Some even slowed down to look at the signs and all the people holding them with smiles on their faces.

One driver came to a stop in front of the homeless with signs and asked, "What are you doing? Do you think anyone will give you money?"

Branyrd stepped forward with a bucket and held it out to the man. "Of course. You will be the first of many who will donate to help those in need. Won't you, sir?"

The man was flustered but opened his wallet and dropped in a five-dollar bill. After meeting Branyrd's sparkling eyes, he pulled out a ten and dropped it in too. He smiled and drove away.

The homeless cheered as they looked inside the can that was no longer empty.

"I can't believe it! You did that, Branyrd. You did something to make him feel guilty if he didn't donate something," Lucas said with elation.

Everyone was patting Branyrd on the back at her success. She smiled and waved her hands over all to calm them down. They were jumping up and down and dancing around with joy for the first time in a long while.

"This is only the beginning. We will have many more who will come forward to help. I assure you. Now hold up those signs high and smile," Branyrd instructed.

More cars came by and slowed down, some stopped and donated while other drivers shook their heads in disbelief.

As the day passed into night, Branyrd told everyone it was time to retire. She would make sure they all had something to eat. She pulled out a basket full of all kinds of bagels, muffins and such and passed them out to everyone. She brought along some thermos bottles of coffee and water too out of thin air. They were amazed at what she could do and oohed and aahed at it all. Some asked her if she was a magician conjuring things out of thin air.

"No, I am not a magician. Everything I do is with HIS help. I cannot do anything without HIS assistance. Always remember that. You cannot do anything without HIM. If you need his support all you have to do is ask. HE will comfort you and guide you always. That is why I am here to help HIM do all HE can for you." Right after this Branyrd once again followed HIS instructions and waved her hands over everyone so they would forget what she just did.

"You have done so much in a short time, Branyrd. We need to do something for you too," Fred stated with a serious expression.

"You are doing a lot to help me. By carrying these signs every day and getting donations will help me reach the goal to purchase these stores. Once we acquire the funds we will be able to work on the stores and get things moving. All we need is help along the way to make it all possible. Are you ready to do that, everyone?"

"Yes!" Everyone chorused together. "We will do anything you ask of us, Branyrd!"

"Thank you. That is all I will need to be successful in my mission."

"I guess that is what we are, a mission," Harold spoke up boldly. "Does HE give you a gold star if you are successful?"

Branyrd turned to look at Harold. "No gold star but wings."

"Wings? You have wings?" Harold asked in shock.

"Yes, all Angels have wings. Each mission we complete will make our wings larger, whiter, stronger and more brilliant than ever before."

"Wow! Can I see your wings, Branyrd?" Ezra asked in wide-eyed wonder.

"Well, no. No one can see my wings, only other Angels in Heaven. That is where my wings materialize. I do not have them on Earth. Sorry."

"But how did you get here? Did you fly without wings?" Ezra couldn't stop from asking.

"No, I had help getting here from my Guardian Angel."

As if on cue Benedicto appeared in front of the crowd. "Hello, everyone. I am Benedicto." He bowed to the men, women, and children.

"Oh, my you are a large man, Benedicto," one woman announced as she gawked at him.

"Yes, I am large for a man. But if you saw me in Heaven, I am larger than this, much larger."

"Really?" Ezra came closer to Benedicto and stood next to the Guardian Angel pulling up his frame to make himself bigger.

"Well, young man. You certainly are a big boy and will be taller soon. How old are you, Ezra?"

Ezra smiled and answered, "I am four. My birthday is coming soon. Right, Daddy?"

"Yes, Ezra. It is in a couple of months in fact."

"Will I have a party?"

"We'll see. We will talk about that later, okay?"

Branyrd looked at Benedicto and smiled. They were planning something inside their heads already for this special little boy.

Branyrd's phone suddenly rang bringing everyone's voices to a halt.

"Yes, this is Branyrd. Wait a minute. I will get him for you."

She looked around and called out, "Lucas, this call is for you."

"Oh, thank you. It must be Cam. He said he would call me back to let me know if he was successful."

"Hi Cam. Yes. Okay. That's great! Let me ask Branyrd when she wants to meet with everyone."

Lucas held the phone against his chest as he whispered to Branyrd, "When do you want to meet my Marine buddies. They are all excited to help and want to get started wherever you need them."

"Okay. Perfect! Tell them to come here tomorrow at noontime. We will make our plans then."

Lucas relayed Branyrd's words and handed the phone back to the Angel.

"Things are looking up, huh, Branyrd?" Fred said. "I'm ready to help my fellow Marines too."

"Thank you, Fred. I appreciate your kindness. I will have plenty for you to do."

"My pleasure, Angel," Fred bowed, patted his chest in thanks to Branyrd and retired to his tent.

"I think it is time for everyone to get a good night's sleep. Did you get enough to eat?"

"Yes," everyone answered. Several said 'thank you' as they went back to their sleeping areas with full and contented stomachs for once.

Branyrd smiled and waved at everyone as she headed back down the alleyway to set up the box bedroom once again for one sleepy-looking little boy and his father.

She guided Ezra and his father inside the warm, safe and comfortable box bedroom for a second night. She kissed Ezra on the head and walked out. She smiled when she saw the boy was already fast asleep with his father cuddling him in his arms and the book sitting on Ezra's chest with his hand holding it protectively.

Benedicto was outside the tent waiting for Branyrd. "Clever box bedroom, Branyrd. I had to see it up close for myself. You really did this all by yourself?"

"I guess so. But I did ask the LORD to help me come up with something for them to be safe."

"Well, you did a great job, little Angel. I'm proud of you."

"Thank you, Benedicto," Branyrd said and blushed at the compliment.

"Tell me about what you plan to do now?" Benedicto inquired.

Branyrd explained what she had done so far with the signs. "We've collected about a hundred dollars so far. I also plan to call the store owners once again. Mr. Poster said he would get back to me soon. I think he may be on board."

"That's good to hear, Branyrd. You have to convince one of the store owners so they will all come forward."

"Yep, that's what I said to Mr. Poster. I hope it works."

"You know you have my help and that of the LORD. You can't go wrong."

"Right, but I want to do this on my own. I know I can do it. I have to convince the owners of these stores and the other stores on the next blocks to come forward and help. If they all help, they can make a difference to so many homeless."

"I agree with you, Branyrd. I know you can do this. But just remember, there is a timeline to complete this mission. It will be getting shorter each day."

"What? How long do I have to complete it, Benedicto? I had a long time for my first mission. HE can't call me back yet. We just got here!"

"No, not yet, little Angel. But HE wants you to try to work faster and complete it. HE doesn't want too many people to know about you being an Angel. It could cause some problems."

"Oh, I see. Maybe I have been too free saying I am an Angel."

"Maybe."

CHAPTER TWELVE

Word was getting around the city that something was up at the homeless camp on Ashley Street. The news channels were sending along some of their people to check it out.

Traffic was picking up in the area too as more cars slowed down to read the signs the homeless were holding and waving around. Several of the homeless were holding out buckets for donations as Branyrd had instructed. She was busy on the phone talking to the owners once again. Mr. Poster promised he would get back to her later that afternoon. He had to speak with his lawyers first about the property.

Branyrd said a prayer as she looked skyward and smiled. "Okay, I will do that, LORD."

Benedicto appeared by her side and asked, "Did HE give you the okay to proceed?"

"Well, yes and no. HE told me to keep quiet about the Angel talk and convince people to do the right thing. HE said I am doing a tremendous job. How do you like that, Benedicto?"

"Wow, that is the highest compliment from on high you could get, Branyrd. Good for you, little Angel."

Branyrd watched the homeless as they waved the signs in front of the traffic which continued to grow. Now there were news station vans pulling up all around them and people with mikes and cameras heading their way.

"What are we going to do, Benedicto? Look at them. They can't wait to get news. But at least this is good news, helping the homeless."

"Yes, it certainly is, Angel. Keep quiet about who you are though. I don't think HE would appreciate it being in the news."

"I know, Benedicto. I know. HE already told me that. I think I can share what we are trying to do here though, right?" Branyrd turned to look for Benedicto when he didn't answer her. Of course, he was no longer there.

A woman stepped onto the sidewalk to get closer to Branyrd but keeping a safe distance from the homeless as if they were contagious. The reporter stuck a mike in front of the Angel's face and asked, after fixing her hair, smoothing out her shirt and putting a wide smile on her pretty face, "Who are you and what are you doing here?"

Branyrd cleared her throat and spoke up with confidence and a serious expression on her face, "My name is Branyrd. I am here to help the homeless in any way I can."

"Who sent you to do this deed?"

"Someone who would rather remain anonymous," she responded as she matched the smile of the reporter.

"Hmm, I see. What do you plan to do to help these homeless people?"

"Well, as you can see, we are seeking donations."

"I noticed the traffic has increased here and people are stopping to donate. That is quite a surprise!"

"Yes, it is, but a good one, don't you think?" Branyrd's smile grew wider with pleasure.

"How do you plan to use these donations? There are many homeless here. Are you planning on feeding them?"

"Well, I am already doing that. But, no, these donations are for a bigger plan which will come to fruition soon."

"Can you share your plan with us?" the reporter looked toward the camera and waited for Branyrd to respond.

"Well, it is not completed yet. I guess I can share some of it with you and your followers out there in cyber land." Branyrd looked toward the camera as if she could see who was watching her.

"I'm sure our watchers would love to hear your plan."

"Umm, yes. I plan to raise funds to purchase the storefronts that are abandoned and refurbish them into places for the homeless to sleep, eat, socialize, and receive medical care."

"That is a mighty big plan you have, Branyrd. Have you ever done anything like this before?" the reporter furrowed her brows in disbelief.

"Not exactly. But I have had a mission before that was quite tough and I completed it in a satisfactory manner."

"A mission in a satisfactory manner, you say? Where do you come from speaking like this?"

"I come from Hea...Haven."

"Is that in Massachusetts?" the reported queried.

"Umm, yes, it is," Branyrd crossed her fingers and looked up to Heaven and apologized in a whisper, *Sorry, Lord.*

"What did you say, Branyrd?"

"Oh, nothing."

Before the reporter could ask another question, an argument arose behind them.

Branyrd excused herself and went over to the tent in question which was moving around and ready to blow away.

"What's the problem here?" Branyrd asked as she poked her head inside the tent. She looked behind her to see if the reporter was following her. So far, she wasn't.

One elderly woman spoke up, "He tried to take some of the money out of my bucket and put into his, Branyrd."

Branyrd looked at the two who were arguing and said in a calming voice, "It doesn't matter how much each of you receive in donations. They are all going into one bucket at the end of the day."

"Okay, the man answered. I was only trying to help Gloria. I think she was taking some of the money out and putting it into her own pockets."

Branyrd focused on the elderly woman who appeared to shrink in front of her. "Did you do that, Glora?"

"Oh no, I didn't do that. I… at least I didn't take too much. I just wanted to get something to eat and a new blanket. My blanket is all ripped and worn."

"Let me see your blanket, Gloria," Branyrd stated as she held out her hands.

Gloria went back to her own tent and pulled out her soiled and ripped blanket that had so many holes in it she could barely hold it together and handed it to the Angel.

"Here is it, Branyrd. See, I told you it was holey," Gloria giggled. "I don't mean that kind of holy though."

Branyrd smiled at Gloria and got the joke. She held the blanket up and prayed. When she had finished her prayer, she put the blanket into Gloria's hands freshly washed and whole once more.

"How did you do that, Branyrd? It smells so good now and is like brand new." Gloria ran around to each of her fellow homeless and let them smell her new blanket. They all praised Branyrd and wanted her to do the same thing to their belongings that were in much need of washing and mending. She planned to do that for all of them soon.

Branyrd quieted down the crowd before the reporter could come over and ask more questions about what she had just done.

Turning to Gloria, Branyrd asked, "Do you have something you want to give me?"

Gloria bent her head in shame and reached into her pocket pulling out a few bills. She handed them over to the Angel and bowed to her.

"No need to bow to me, Gloria. Thank you for returning what was not yours. Remember what I am doing here is for all of you. It will benefit everyone who needs help."

"Yes, Branyrd. I am so sorry," Gloria apologized and bent over in a coughing fit and collapsed at the Angel's feet.

Witnessing this, the reporter rushed over with her cameraman in tow to find out what happened.

"Is she all right, Branyrd? What did she do?"

"She will be fine. I need to get her back to her tent." Branyrd lifted the woman up as if she weighed nothing and walked over to the nearby tent and placed Gloria inside.

The reporter waited outside the tent at a safe distance and whispered to her cameraman. "Go around the back of the tent and try to get a view of what Branyrd is doing."

"Okay." He moved stealthily with his camera close to his side.

Inside Branyrd was saying a prayer over Gloria. She could hear a deep rattle inside the woman's chest. It didn't sound like she would have much time left. The Angel prayed HE would not take Gloria yet. Branyrd wanted Gloria to be there when the mission was completed.

HE announced, "You cannot keep everyone there, Branyrd. Some of them will be leaving before you. It is Gloria's time. I will not take her yet, but soon."

"Oh no," Branyrd felt Gloria's pain and wiped away her tears as she laid her hands on the woman's forehead and chest to help her breath easier and take away the pain with the LORD's guidance.

The cameraman made a noise that alerted Branyrd. She came out of the tent and pulled him back from it. "What are you doing there? This woman is very sick. Please give her some respect and space." Branyrd's eyes glowed as she looked at the man. He nearly dropped his camera when he met her stare.

"So sorry. I didn't know she was that sick." He backed away holding tightly to his camera and went to speak with the reporter.

"What's going on in there?" she asked her cameraman. He shook his head and pulled the reporter away. "That woman is very sick. I think we should leave. Maybe it's contagious."

"Oh my! Okay. I guess we have enough for now," the reporter said as they hurried away to their van.

Branyrd sighed in relief that they were gone. She hadn't wanted them to see what she had done to Gloria's blanket or that Gloria was now walking around appearing to be a picture of health for now anyway.

She felt a vibration in her pocket and realized it was her phone.

CHAPTER THIRTEEN

"Hello. Yes, this is Branyrd. Okay. That would be great, Mr. Poster. See you soon."

Branyrd was all smiles when she turned to face the tents and their occupants. "I've got great news, everyone!"

"What is it, Branyrd," Gloria came forward first.

"Listen up, everyone. Mr. Poster is on his way here with his lawyers. He is going to sign the building over to us. He has some contingencies we must agree to before he will sign."

"Hurray!" Gloria cried out and others joined in.

Fred asked, "What contingencies?"

"I don't know that yet. We will find out soon. He is on his way here now. Everyone, return to your tents. Clear out any mess in front of your places. We want to make a good impression."

Everyone cleared out any debris and went back into their tents until told otherwise by Branyrd.

Branyrd collected the donations that were now slowing down to a trickle. She smiled and thanked every driver who stopped and donated. Even some of the news station vans came over to donate hoping to get something newsworthy to report to their bosses.

A few large vans came forward and pulled up to the place where Branyrd was standing. The doors opened and many men came out and nodded to her. Some were in uniforms fatigues while others were in jeans and sweats.

Behind her she heard Lucas's voice, "Hey everyone. Thanks for coming! We really need your help!"

The men stepped aside to let Lucas come forward. He turned to Branyrd and said, "These are my fellow Marines. They are here to do whatever you need them to do." He waved his hands around introducing Branyrd to the men, "This is Branyrd. She is a savior to all the homeless. She has big plans to change this street and help us all find a place where we will be accepted and once again be able to gain our independence and respect."

The men cleared their throats and said, "Nice to meet you, Branyrd," several times over. They shook her hand and waited for her to respond.

"It's a pleasure to meet all of you, thank you so much for being here. We will need every one of you to make this plan possible. Did Lucas lay out the plan for you?"

Lucas responded, "Yes, I did, but I'm sure you have much more to share with them. I only told them what you want to do with the storefronts. I didn't know what else you had in mind. They are strong, willing, and able to help."

"That is most kind of you," Branyrd said with a benevolent smile that covered everyone with a warm feeling.

The Marines whispered amongst themselves and waited for more instructions. They shuffled their feet and appeared to be anxious to get started. They stood at attention as if they were still in the service, force of habit.

Before Branyrd could share more with them another black SUV pulled up and parked behind the other vans. She waited to see if this was the person she was expecting.

"Are you Branyrd?" a small middle-aged man with a bald pate and glasses stepped forward with his hand outstretched." I am Marvin Poster."

Branyrd met him half-way. "Yes, I'm Branyrd. It's a pleasure to meet you, Mr. Poster."

"Marvin, please. Call me Marvin. May I call you Branyrd since I don't know your last name?"

"Oh, yes, of course, Marvin. Call me Branyrd."

Two men were directly behind Marvin wearing serious expressions, pinstriped suits and dark glasses. Branyrd glanced their way and smiled. This made them relax a little and come closer.

Marvin coughed and said, "Sorry, these two men are my lawyers. You can probably see by their expressions of displeasure that they do not want me to do this."

"I see. What are you planning to do, Marvin? We didn't actually discuss this in detail yet. You mentioned some contingencies."

Marvin tried to clear his throat and coughed again this time deeper and more lasting as he bent over in discomfit.

"Are you all right, Marvin? Can I get you a drink of water?"

"No, I'm okay. I have a bottle in my pocket. Let me take a drink and then we can continue."

"Of course. Take your time," Branyrd said as she watched Marvin struggling to gain his voice even after a drink from his water bottle.

The lawyers moved closer to Marvin and held his arms to support him. Their faces looked even more pinched in dismay as they stood next to their client.

Branyrd met one of the lawyer's eye and he shook his head. She whispered in the man's ear, "Is he sick?"

The lawyer nodded and avoided looking at Branyrd as his eyes filled.

"I'm sorry to hear that," she sighed.

"I'm all right, Branyrd," Marvin said as he regained his composure and voice. "Carter always worries about everything," he said, pointing to the man to his right. "Now let's get down to business, shall we?"

Branyrd responded in a calming voice and took his arm to help Marvin feel better. He immediately looked at Branyrd and spoke in a clear voice, strong with conviction.

"Hmm, that's strange. I feel much better suddenly. My voice is no longer hoarse." Marvin shook his head in wonder. "Whatever just happened, I am thankful. Did you do something, Branyrd?"

"Oh, no. The water must have helped you, Marvin. Let me get you a seat so you don't tax yourself any more than necessary."

Marvin nodded and sat in a chair which suddenly appeared out of a nearby tent.

"Are you comfortable, Marvin?" Branyrd enquired.

"Umm, yes, surprisingly so. Thank you, Branyrd. Now let me see. You asked me about contingencies, did you not?"

"Yes, I did. What must I do to meet these contingencies and what are they?"

"Well, nothing too difficult to do. You must promise that this storefront will always be kept in good condition inside and out. No garbage is allowed anywhere on the sidewalk in front of the store. I'm sure you have plans to paint and fix it up a little before using it, right?"

"Most definitely, Marvin. I already have plenty of help here waiting to begin the clean up and repair." Branyrd looked toward the group of Marines who were standing close by with Lucas waiting for instructions.

Marvin followed Branyrd's eyes and noted the group of men. "They certainly look more than capable to handle any task you throw at them, Branyrd. They look like servicemen. Are they?"

"Yes, they are former Marines."

"Impressive, very impressive. I always wanted to go into the service but, alas, I was 4F with my breathing problems." He waved and saluted to the group who did the same in return.

"Is there anything else that we must do for contingencies, Marvin?"

"Well, there is one more thing. Will you be in charge of this store or will you be signing it over to someone else?"

Branyrd searched for Lucas and beckoned him closer. "This man is Lucas and his son, Ezra. He will be in charge once this store is operational. Of course, I need to get all the other store owners on board before I can complete the renovations."

Lucas met Branyrd's eyes and questioned, "What? You want me to do this? Where are you going, Branyrd?"

"I have other missions to complete and can't stay here once this plan is finished."

"But, how can I do all this? I don't know what to do."

"I will make sure you know exactly what needs to be done, Lucas. I trust in you and your fellow Marines to complete everything before I have to leave."

"But…"

Branyrd waved his protests away and patted Lucas on the shoulder. "You will be fine, don't worry."

CHAPTER FOURTEEN

Marvin instructed his lawyers to prepare the paperwork for signatures. They pulled out a valise and placed the papers for the transfer of property on top.

"Now, Branyrd. This is the property you will be taking over. You need to sign here and here."

"What about payment? How much do you want for this property, Marvin? I have some donations that need to be totaled. I'm not sure if we have enough yet."

"No need for any payment. I am giving you this place free and clear. I don't need the money. I have more than enough and besides I can't take it with me where I am going," he chuckled.

"What? Where are you going, Marvin?" Branyrd didn't like the sound of this.

"I hope to be going to a place to be with my wife. She passed away several years ago. She has been waiting for me for a long time."

Branyrd jerked forward and gripped Marvin's hand. "You can't be saying you are dying?" She realized as much but didn't want to believe it.

"Yes, Branyrd. I am, and have been for the past few years. I know it is my time. I have done enough over my lifetime but need to do this one thing before I am called."

"But you can get a doctor to help you."

"No, they cannot do anything more for me. It's okay, Branyrd. Don't look so distressed. I am fine with it. I miss my Marian so much. It's been difficult being without her all these years. I don't know why HE took her first. I should have gone first," he sighed heavily as his eyes brimmed with tears.

Branyrd held onto Marvin's hands and squeezed them as she said a prayer. *Please don't take him yet, LORD!*

She heard HIS voice in her head, "It is his time, Branyrd. He is a good man and wants to do something good before he is taken. He has earned a place with me."

Branyrd held her breath and rubbed her eyes that were tear-filled as much as Marvin's. She gave the man a hug and said, "Thank you for your kindness. What you are doing will help the homeless for a long time, Marvin. I am sure you will be repaid in Heaven for your generosity ten-fold."

"I hope HE will look upon me and accept this sinner and forgive my errant ways."

"I think HE already has, Marvin. HE already has."

"Do you have some connections, Branyrd," he giggled as he met her eyes, but when he saw her expression and the light that emanated behind her, he was startled.

"Hmm, who knows?" Branyrd tittered in response.

The lawyers laid out the papers and got both parties to sign. Branyrd had Lucas sign on the same line as her signature. She planned on changing that before she left though. Her signature would disappear eventually leaving Lucas as the sole owner.

"Well, that was easy enough," Marvin said in relief.

"Yes, it was, Marvin. We can't thank you enough for your generosity and kindness toward these men and women. You may have saved many of their lives."

"I hope I save someone in the process. It is the least I can do," Marvin smiled and shook Branyrd's hand in closing the deal. He handed her copies of everything and waved and saluted the Marines in passing as he walked back to his SUV with his two lawyers in tow.

Before entering his vehicle, he turned to Branyrd and said, "Goodbye, Branyrd. Good luck to you all."

"Take care and may God bless you, Marvin. Thank you again."

CHAPTER FIFTEEN

Branyrd had the Marines get right to work inside and outside the storefront that now belonged to them. She sent a couple of Marines to the hardware store down the next few blocks to get all the supplies they would need to paint and repair the place. When the Marines returned, they handed back the money Branyrd had given them to make the purchases saying, "The store manager wouldn't take our money. She said it was on the house."

Branyrd nodded and smiled. "That was kind of her."

As the Marines were working on the store, Branyrd phoned the rest of the store owners to let them know she now owned one of the stores in the middle, and tried to convince them to do the same thing as Marvin. They were still holding out even after much cajoling on her part. She would give them a few days and try again.

She had Lucas count the money on hand to see how much there was available for a down payment for at least one of the stores. He came back with the amount which was well short of what they would need. The Angel put Lucas in charge of keeping the money in a safe place until needed.

Branyrd looked up to Heaven and prayed, "What can we do, LORD. You don't want me to ask for your intercession, do you?"

"No, Branyrd. I know you can do this on your own without my help. I know you will figure out a way to make it all work out. Time is of the essence, Angel. You must complete this mission soon. I will have Benedicto let you know how much time you have left. I believe in you!"

The Angel sighed and used her mind to figure out what to do next without HIS help. If HE believed in her, she had to believe in herself.

She called out to her Guardian Angel, Benedicto, for his counsel, "Where are you, Benedicto? I need your assistance."

"Ahh, Angel. Here I am. I am always close by. You don't have to yell. You only have to think of me or whisper my name and I will come."

"Okay, Benedicto. I understand. Now, please help me. What am I to do? How will I get enough money to buy more of the stores? We aren't getting enough with the donations. We only have under a thousand dollars. This is not going to be enough to do anything other than fix up the outside of the place and clean the street in front."

"Yes, I can see that. But you do have plenty of help from the Marines and the homeless too. You must put all of them to work. After all, it is for them you do this."

"I know, but some of them are old, feeble and too ill to do much. I have helped some of them get back on their feet but for how long? HE said he would be taking some of them soon. I want them to see this come to fruition before they are taken."

"Yes, I understand, little Angel. I think HE does too. HE knows how persistent you are and that you will complete this mission in due time before HE takes any of them."

"HE told me, you will let me know how long I have left to complete my mission. Do you know how long I have?"

"Well, HE will tell me soon, I'm sure. I don't know anything about that yet. Be patient, Branyrd. I will help you if you need me."

Branyrd sighed and said, "Thank you, Benedicto." But there was no one there to hear her words.

Lucas came over to her and asked, "Did you realize that you put my name on the deed? I can't be responsible for all this. I don't know the first thing about handling property like this. Besides, I begin work at the Safety-First Hardware Store tomorrow."

"Yes, I remembered, Lucas. But you will be the caretaker of all this when I must leave. Don't concern yourself with it yet. When I need you to take over completely, I will let you know."

"But…"

Branyrd waved her hands over Lucas to calm him down and turned her attention to the Marines who were working on the store. It was looking brighter, cleaner and ready for inspection.

"Lucas, let's go check inside to see how it's coming along. We have to figure out what we will use this store for – sleeping, café or clinic.

"I don't think it's big enough to use for sleeping quarters," Lucas said as he looked around the floor space. "It might be okay for medical care though. We have room for several beds for the sick and we can put in a closet for medical supplies here and desks and chairs for the doctor and nurse to keep track of patients."

Branyrd smiled as she listened to Lucas take charge as she knew he was more than capable of doing.

"Hi Daddy and Branyrd," Ezra announced as he came to see what they were doing. "I've been helping your friends, Daddy, do some painting. I can do the bottom while they reach the top of the walls. Look, I did all that over there already."

"Yes, I see you did a great job, Ezra. Congratulations, son! I am so proud of you. It looks like you have paint all over you. We'll have to buy you some new clothes."

"It's okay, Daddy. We can wash them, can't we?" Ezra looked at Branyrd for help.

"No problem, Ezra. I'll take care of that. You go finish up and we will see you later. Good job!"

Branyrd went around to each worker and patted them on the back. "Great job, everyone. It looks like a brand-new place. Do we have any carpenters here?"

One Marine stepped forward and said, "I do a lot of woodworking and have done so since I was just a kid. My father taught me everything he knows. What do you need, Branyrd?"

"Well, let's see. You should check with Lucas he has the ideas already planned out. Right, Lucas?"

Lucas smiled and nodded to his fellow Marine, "Yes. We need to draw up the plans, Nick. Come over here and let's use this floor space to draw up what I think would work for this place to be perfect for a medical facility for all."

CHAPTER SIXTEEN

The next day Lucas began his first day at his new job. He left Ezra in the care of his fellow homeless. Branyrd had promised to keep a watch over his son too in between her supervision of the work on the store.

Amy spent the better part of the morning instructing Lucas about their inventory and store. He listened and learned as much as he could.

"What do you think, Lucas? Do you think you are going to enjoy working here?" Amy asked, closely watching his reaction.

"Well, I learned a lot more than I thought today from you and your staff. I thought I knew more about this stuff. But I guess I was wrong."

"No, you were not wrong, Lucas. You knew most of it already. I see that you were in the Marines."

"Yes, four years." Lucas didn't add any more information.

"Was it difficult?" Amy watched Lucas's face pale as he turned away from her and busied himself with stocking a shelf.

"I will understand if you don't want to talk about it, Lucas. I'm sorry for asking. I'll let you get back to work. Don't forget to stop for lunch. It's almost that time now."

Lucas nodded as he finished up emptying a case filled with boxes of nails and stacking them. He turned to look for Amy but she had gone back to the cash register to talk to a customer.

He shook his head and thought, how can I share what I went through with anyone? It was too horrendous for me to even think about. The nightmares won't leave me. Why would I want to give someone like Amy these horrific things to think about?

As he turned to go to the lunchroom, he met Amy's eyes as she smiled at him. He tried to smile back but couldn't.

There were a few other staff in the room and they introduced themselves and showed Lucas how to use the soda and sandwich machines. They even left some change out in case he needed it.

"Thanks, guys. I appreciate it. I didn't bring any change with me. I will repay you when I get paid, I promise."

"No problem, we share here. We are like family. Nice to meet you, Lucas."

"Likewise," Lucas said as the men left the lunch room to return to work.

Lucas looked at the choices for lunch and drinks. There were several to choose from. He couldn't believe there were any at all. He had never met such kind people before, said a prayer of thanks for everything he had received since Branyrd had come into his life, and sat down to enjoy his sandwich and drink.

Amy stopped by to get a cup of coffee and took the seat next to Lucas. "I'm sorry, Lucas, about before."

"Nothing to be sorry about, Amy. I just can't talk about my years in the Marines. It wasn't pleasant."

"I can't imagine, Lucas. You don't have to share any of it. Please don't think about it. Okay?"

"Maybe one day I will be able to think about that time in my life without having nightmares."

"You have nightmares?" Amy asked before she could stop herself.

"Yes, too many. But I am working on getting through it all."

"That's good to hear, Lucas. Whatever I can do to help you. Please let me know." Amy sipped her coffee and watched Lucas as he finished his lunch and got up to excuse himself.

"Well, I better get back to work or my boss will fire me," he smirked as he smiled at Amy and left the room.

Amy sat there for a few more minutes and sighed. She said to herself, "I wish I could help him. He is such a nice man, probably the nicest one I have met in a long time."

Lucas was thinking somewhere along the same line about Amy being the nicest woman he had met since his wife.

The day passed quickly for Lucas as he grabbed his jacket and stopped to say good bye to Amy and the rest of the staff.

"I can't believe it's that time already, Lucas. How did you like your first day? You did an excellent job stocking shelves and helping customers. You fit right in with the other clerks too. They all like you."

"Oh, thanks, Amy. You have a good business here and friendly and welcoming staff. They made me feel right at home, especially in the lunch room. They even paid for my lunch. I'll have to buy lunch for them in return."

"Good to hear. Listen, Lucas, we had a few donations in your box today. Do you want to take it with you to give to your group who are working on the plans?"

"Wow! You got a lot of cash in there, Amy? Who donated all that? I didn't even see anyone putting anything in there."

"Well, some of your fellow co-workers heard about what you are doing for the homeless and wanted to help. I also added a little something in there too. That is the least we can do to help. When you do this, it helps all of us."

"Thank you, Amy. Thank everyone who donated. I can't wait to show Branyrd how much you collected in one day. She will be thrilled."

"Branyrd? Who is Branyrd?" Amy asked with a frown.

"Oh, she is the one who is doing all this to help the homeless. I am one of them but soon I won't be."

"Is she your girlfriend?"

"No, no nothing like that. She is an...a friend of the homeless. She came here to help. I don't understand why but we are all grateful to her and can never repay her for what she is doing to help us."

"I see. I would like to meet this... woman. Maybe I will stop by later today. Will she be there tonight?"

"Probably. She never leaves until everyone is settled down for the night. I don't even know where she is staying. She even feeds us."

"Wow, that is incredible. How does she do all this? And why?"

"That is a good question, Amy. Maybe when you stop by you can ask Branyrd."

"Maybe I will, Lucas. See you later."

***

Amy closed the store and walked the few blocks to see what was going on. There were others out and about checking out what was going on in the homeless community.

She was looking forward to meeting this woman who was doing all this to help the homeless. She couldn't imagine why anyone would do this. It was an enormous task to undertake. She was also intrigued to see if she had any competition for Lucas's attention.

CHAPTER SEVENTEEN

Branyrd was getting everyone settled for the night when a large car drove up to the curb in front of her. She couldn't see inside because of the blackened windows, but soon the doors opened and out came Mayor Cramston.

"Well, Branyrd, I see you have been busy here. It is looking better, I must say," the mayor exclaimed in surprise.

"Thank you, Mayor. Good to see you again."

"Did you file a work order, a permit, with the city planner about your renovations? You must do that before you begin. About the donations you are getting here, you cannot solicit on the street like this. It is not acceptable."

"No, we haven't gotten a permit but we will do that right away. I wasn't aware of that. About the donations, we are not doing anything to coerce anyone into donating. It is purely their own choice."

"Hmm, I see. Well, it doesn't look good for my city. I will not tolerate it. You must cease and desist immediately. Do you understand, Branyrd?"

"Yes, of course. We will stop right away. Sorry, Mayor Cramston. I didn't realize it was not acceptable. It is not harming anyone, I assure you. In fact, it is bringing more people into your city."

"Yes, I notice that. It isn't always a good thing though. What you are doing will only encourage more homeless to come to my city. That I do not want."

"On the contrary, Mayor Cramston. I think we are only encouraging more people to come settle here and purchase stores and frequent this place once it is back to normal."

"How do you plan to do all this? You did promise to share your plans with me?"

"I'm sorry, Mayor, I have been so busy I didn't get back to see you. I can explain it all to you now. Would you like to see what we have done to one store already?"

"Did you purchase it with the donations?" he asked, in disbelief.

"No, we did not have enough donations to do that. Mr. Poster was kind enough to donate his store to our cause for the homeless."

"What? Old man Poster gave you his store free and clear? I don't believe it!"

"Well, he did. He was kind enough to do that. I can't ever repay him for his generosity, but it will help save many."

"Interesting. I never saw Poster do a kind thing in his life. I wonder what came over him? When he lost his wife, he became a recluse and even more miserly," the mayor mused.

"I think he had his reasons, Mayor. He is a kind man. He misses his wife."

"I don't know about kindness. Though he does miss his wife, I'm sure. I have known Poster my whole life. We grew up together in this city which was just a town at the time. He worked hard and bought every store in town as soon as he could. He wanted to own the town. He and I had our arguments about that. I thought he was trying to buy his way into becoming the mayor. But I guess he had other things he wanted more."

"Maybe he realized there is more to life than owning property," Branyrd stated.

"Well...maybe. Now that you own the store, what are you going to do with it?"

Branyrd beckoned the mayor to follow her. She entered the store and waved her hands around to show him what had been completed so far.

"Well, well, look at this. It looks like a clinic of some kind. You have beds and desks and shelves and closets. What are you going to do with it?"

"Yes, it is a clinic for the homeless to use. This is only the beginning, Mayor Cramston."

"Where are you going to get doctors and nurses to run this? Who is going to pay for the expenses all this will incur?" He smirked at Branyrd.

Branyrd met his smirk with a smile. "I have plans for all this. Don't worry, Mayor Cramston. I have plans I will share with you as soon as they are completed."

"I look forward to hearing about these so-called plans, Branyrd. I hope they won't cause my city any other problems."

"No, they won't. I promise you. Well, I think it is time for me to make sure everyone is safely tucked inside their tents until I come back tomorrow. See you later, Mayor Cramston."

"Hmm. Good night, Branyrd. I will be back again to check on your progress. Don't forget what I said about the begging for donations. That is not allowed here."

"Of course. I understand, Mayor. There will not be any more requests for donations."

After the mayor left Branyrd sighed heavily. What was she going to do now? The mayor made it extremely clear he did not tolerate soliciting for donations. She was deep in thought and didn't see the young woman coming toward her until she heard a voice.

"Are you Branyrd?"

"Yes. Do I know you?"

"No, I'm Amy from Safety First Hardware Store. I heard about what you are doing for the homeless. It's incredible and kind of you to donate your time like this for them.

Others have tried and failed. I hope you will be successful for all of our sakes."

"Thank you, Amy. I heard about you too from Lucas and Ezra. Ezra is quite taken with you. He is such a sweet boy."

"Oh, I love little Ezra. He is an adorable little guy. I fell in love with him the minute I met him and he opened his mouth to tell me about his father needing a job. Who wouldn't give him anything he requested. I certainly couldn't refuse him."

"Yes, I know what you mean, Amy. I felt the same way."

"Umm, do you like Lucas?"

"Of course, he is a good man."

"Yes, I agree." Amy looked down at her feet when she felt her cheeks blush.

"How did Lucas do on his first day? Did he enjoy working in your store?" Branyrd tried to make Amy comfortable when she noticed her flushed cheeks. She didn't mention Lucas had told her he was happy at his job and looked forward to going back the next day.

"He seemed to enjoy it, did well in everything I gave him to do and got along well with his co-workers."

"That's good to know. Listen, Amy. I am not staying around after this is all done. I have plans to go elsewhere to help others, and I am not romantically-interested in Lucas."

"Oh, I didn't mean to infer anything about that. I...I don't even know if he is married."

"Well, he is married but estranged from his wife. Maybe he should tell you about it. It's not my place to discuss this."

"Okay. I...I don't know what to say. I'm sorry for bothering you. But I was curious about what you are doing here. You are to be commended on all this. It's incredible! Things are looking better already. Is there anything I can do to help?"

"You have already done a lot for us, Amy. I must thank you for the supplies you sent us with the Marines. They said you wouldn't take their money, and for the donations you collected and added to at your store. We appreciate your kindness."

"Well, it's the least I could do for the community. We have all suffered with the homeless taking over the neighborhood like this. I know they can't help it but it has drained our city."

"That is why I am here to do all I can to change that."

"We are fortunate you came. I want to help in any way I can. What do you want me to do?"

"Well, you could spread word about what we are doing here with the other businesses where you are and further away. That would help."

"Yes, that would be perfect. I will send around a flyer to tell them what you are doing here and that you need all the help you can get to rebuild our city."

"Awesome idea, Amy! Thank you so much. Would you like to see what we have done so far with one of the stores?"

"I'd love to see it."

Amy was in awe of the work that was done inside the soon-to-be clinic. She looked closely at the shelves, floors, beds and desks all handmade by the Marines.

"This is incredible work! Who did this?"

"We have some of Lucas's fellow Marines working on this place."

"I could use these guys to do some remodeling for my store. I'm sure there are other businesses that could use this type of skilled work."

"Well, come back tomorrow and you can ask the Marines about it."

"I certainly will. Nice to meet you, Branyrd. See you soon."

"Thank you, Amy, for stopping by. Nice meeting you too. I look forward to seeing you again."

***

The next day Branyrd went inside to find Lucas and Nick and relay what the mayor said about getting a permit to renovate and buildup the stores.

"I should have known about that," Lucas said as Nick nodded in agreement. "We will take care of it right away."

"Let's take a break now, Nick, and go visit the city planner and get our permit before we get into any other trouble with the mayor."

"Right, let's go. Okay with you, Branyrd?"

"Of course. Thanks, Lucas and Nick, for taking care of this. I don't know about such things," Branyrd shrugged her shoulders and smirked.

CHAPTER EIGHTEEN

The news stations all over the city were running the story about the homeless community and a young woman who is taking on this problem that has been plaguing the city. They said, 'this woman has proven to be a dynamo who even stood up to Mayor Cramston.'

This last sentence had Mayor Cramston fuming in his office. He sputtered and threw the paper into his trash can. "What's going on here? What do they mean she stood up to me? No one tells me what to do. I am the boss of this city and everyone better not forget it! No little woman is going to take away my thunder!"

The mayor's secretary, Alice, came running into his office to see what he was yelling about.

"Do you need me, sir?" Alice's voice shook as she saw her boss's red face and how much he was sweating.

"Get me a cup of joe, Alice, and make it sweet!"

"Yes, Mayor. Right away."

Alice scurried off like a little mouse who was chasing a piece of cheese. She came back in under a minute and handed over the cup of coffee, backing away as quickly as she could.

"Where do you think you are going, Alice? I need you here. Take a letter. I want to tell these idiot newspapers a thing or two about who runs this city. It's not some woman who strolls in with an agenda to change the city. I am the only one who can do that!"

"Yes, sir," Alice nodded and took down the mayor's words.

"Now type it up and bring it back to me pronto. You will hand carry a copy to all the newspaper editors today!"

"I could email them all quicker, sir."

"No! I want you to bring a copy to each of them. You will wait for them to read the letter and then report back to me with their response. I want you to describe what their faces looked like when they read my letter. Do you understand? You can't do that with an email. These stupid computers are worthless to me. They are impersonal and don't allow me the power to see reactions to my words."

Alice shook her head and thought, I need to get another job. This man is crazy and is driving me in the same direction.

The mayor sat and fumed until Alice came in with the copies for him to sign. She went back to her desk and put each letter in an envelope and rushed out to her car to drive to each of the newspaper offices.

***

Branyrd was back to work the next day and supervising everything that still needed to be done. She spoke to the Marines and mentioned they may have another job because of the exemplary woodworking they had completed.

"Thank you, Branyrd. Who is interested in my work?" the Marine queried.

"The Safety-First Hardware Store manager, Amy. I didn't get her last name. She said she would be back sometime today to speak with you about what she needs done."

"Wow, that's great! I have to thank my fellow Marines also for their help. I taught them how to make the shelves and they are quick learners. We may go into business together after this if it pays off. I can't thank you enough, Branyrd. I didn't know what I was going to do for work. I may not be homeless but I was getting close to that without work."

"Happy to help. I'm sorry I don't know your name, Marine. I don't want to keep calling you Marine," Branyrd giggled.

"Oh, sorry, Branyrd. I'm Nick."

"Nice to meet you officially, Nick. I will have to thank all the Marines for their excellent work."

"It's looking pretty good, I have to say too, Branyrd. I had forgotten how much I love woodworking. I think I will be doing a lot more of this kind of work. We are here for as long as you need us. All my fellow Marines agree on that. It's nice to have a purpose again. When we left the Marines we were all despondent and having a difficult time adjusting to civilian life. We have been more fortunate than Lucas though since we did not suffer as much as he did with PTSD. I had to go to a therapist for months after I came back. It helped me a lot to accept things would never be the same."

"I'm sorry for whatever you had to go through during your time, Nick, but I am relieved you have come back stronger with help. If you ever need to talk, I am here to listen. I don't profess to know what it feels like to be in the service but I am empathic and sympathetic to your need to share your angst. Most of all, I thank you for your service to your country. You are to be commended for your sacrifices."

"You are welcome, by the way. I felt I needed to do whatever I could, Branyrd. I hope I made a difference being there. But I need to put a thank you back on you for what you have given us – a new lease on life."

"I think you earned it, Nick. I hope you will have an amazing life from now on with a job you love to do."

"I see that as a possibility now, Branyrd. Thank you."

"Well, I know you have a lot to do yet. We are just beginning. There are many other stores we have to acquire and renovate. Are you up to the task, Nick, you and your fellow Marines?"

"Yes, most definitely, Branyrd. I better get to work. I need to make a few more beds. There are so many people out here that don't look healthy. We need to make room for them."

"Sounds good to me, Nick. Get to work," Branyrd chuckled.

Branyrd made a point to thank each Marine in person for the exemplary work they were doing. They patted their chests in thanks and continued working.

Fred stopped in to look at the store's renovations. He also wanted to speak to his fellow Marines. "Hi guys. Do you need any help here?"

The Marines had all met Fred and were impressed with his sharp intellect for his age. They welcomed him in. "Sure, Fred, we always need the help of a fellow Marine."

Fred couldn't stop smiling. He had not felt useful for a long time and now he had a purpose. He grabbed a hammer and nails and got to work after instructions to what needed to be done.

Gloria was keeping busy bossing everyone around about keeping their areas clean. She stooped down to pick up any trash that flew into the gutters and tossed it into the trash cans Branyrd had supplied.

Harold was scowling as usual and stood watching everyone working. He folded his hands across his chest and humphed about what was being done as if he was the boss.

"What's the problem, Harold?" Branyrd asked as she came closer to him.

"Well, I don't understand why Fred is in there. What does he know about woodworking anyway?" he grumbled.

"Evidently, he does know something, Harold. Would you like to help them too?"

"What? I...umm. Okay." Harold smiled at Branyrd's words.

"Let's get you some tools so you can get started. Okay, Harold?"

"Yup. Okay! I'm ready to help. I am quite handy. Why no one asked me before this though is the question," Harold mumbled, but kept a smile on his face.

Harold couldn't help asking, "Where did you get all these tools? Did you get them for you like she gets everything else?"

Branyrd grinned at Harold and answered, "No, we purchased them with donations and the help of the manager of Safety-First Hardware Store. Amy has been most generous in assisting us in getting them."

"Hmm, I see," Harold grinner, nodded and grabbed a hammer to get to work.

CHAPTER NINETEEN

Alice sighed each time she had to hand a letter to an editor. She tried to keep a straight face as they looked at the letters in shock which quickly turned to anger. She knew photos would have been better than her words to describe the editors' dismay at the mayor's boldness.

She couldn't believe her boss had said 'cease and desist about reporting about the woman who is helping the homeless' to the editors, 'or else.' What did he mean or else?

Alice smiled wanly and walked away after each editor muttered a few choice words. She didn't blame them for being disgruntled and thought the woman helping deserved the commendations that were being awarded to her. She knew the mayor was envious of the attention Branyrd was getting from the public. He was too full of himself as everyone knew.

She got back to the office and went into the mayor's office with the news as he requested.

Mayor Cramston looked up from his phone call and put up a finger to hold Alice off a minute. Once he put the phone down, he smiled at her and said, "Well, how did the little expedition go?"

Alice related what she saw and heard from the editors much to the delight of her boss. He couldn't stop laughing and started choking and couldn't stop. She rushed to his side and offered him a sip of cold coffee.

"Stop, I…," cough…cough, "I don't need any coffee. I'm fine," he finally said after getting his voice back with a deep breath and sigh.

"Are you okay now, Mayor?"

"Yes, yes. Go away now. Don't you have work to do, Alice?"

He shooed her out of his office so he could make a call to the editors. Before he could make the first call his phone rang with one of them calling him.

"Hello. Yes, this is Mayor Cramston. How can I help you?"

"What is the meaning of this letter, Mayor? Who do you think you are telling me what to write. What does 'or else' mean?"

Mayor parried back and forth with some of the words used by the disgruntled editors as more of them called him to discuss his letter.

Mayor Cramston was enjoying getting all the attention once again even if it was negative. He warned the editors, "Be careful what you write. You will not mention this Branyrd woman or the homeless in the same context again. Do you understand? If anyone is to help the homeless then it will be me."

Mayor repeated this mantra to each of the editors in turn and slammed his phone down on the last one. He chuckled because he couldn't have done that with his cell.

Alice heard every word that was being postulated back and forth. She shut off her computer and cleaned out her desk. She had made a decision, probably the best one she could make – she was going to quit.

She knocked on her boss's door and waited to hear his reply.

"Yes? What do you want?"

Alice opened the door and announced, "I quit!"

Before Mayor Cramston could remark she went out the door, left the office with her belongings in a box, and was in the elevator feeling good for the first time about herself.

Alice headed to Ashley Street to see how she could help Branyrd and the homeless despite the mayor.

She tittered to herself as she drove over to begin something worthwhile for a change. She may soon become homeless herself since she was now unemployed.

CHAPTER TWENTY

The Marines were almost finished with the renovations on the store. It was time to get more of the store owners on board. Branyrd picked up her list and began to call them. She wouldn't give up until they agreed to help out as Mr. Poster had so generously done.

As she was trying every tactic she could but unsuccessfully, she looked up from her phone and saw several people standing in front of her waiting to speak to her.

"Hi. What can I do for you? I'm sorry I was busy with business about these stores."

One man stepped forward and said, "We are some of the business owners a few blocks and more away from here. We've come to help you in any way we can."

"Oh, my goodness. Really? That's wonderful! Thank you," Branyrd gushed in surprise.

"We have been reading the newspapers about what you are doing singlehandedly. We want to help," a woman stated with a broad smile.

"Well, I don't know what to say but thank you and welcome aboard."

"I'm Kayden, spokesman for the group. They decided I have a gift for gab. What can we do to help, Branyrd, right?"

"Yes, I'm Branyrd. Well, there is much to do but we are at a stalemate with the other store owners. They don't want to give up their stores or even sell them to us. Of course, we don't have enough money to buy them. The mayor has stopped us from taking donations from the public."

"We know how cantankerous our mayor can be. Let us take care of him. We have ways of getting around his authority with connections that can put pressure on him," Kayden announced.

"Oh no, you can't do anything violent, please!" Branyrd cried out in alarm. She did not want to be responsible for any trouble like that. HE would never forgive her.

"Nothing like that, Branyrd, I assure you," Kayden said with a smile. "We don't plan to be violent, just stubborn and unyielding where it is needed."

"Okay, but you must let me know what you are going to do before you do it. Okay? I feel responsible for anything that happens while I am here."

"No problem, Branyrd. We have work to do and will keep you in the loop. Come on everyone. We need to get started on convincing the mayor that he is wrong."

The group soon dispersed leaving Branyrd in a tizzy. She whispered to HIM, "What am I going to do? I have no idea what they are planning. Can you counsel me and let me know. I don't want them to do anything wrong."

"Don't worry, Angel. I am keeping my eyes on all of them. They have good hearts and only mean to do the right thing. I'm sure they will tell you soon what they plan to do. Keep up the good work, Branyrd."

***

Back at the mayor's office he was yelling for help now that he didn't have a secretary. Other people from the adjoining offices came in to see what he was complaining about more than normal.

"What's going on, Mayor?" the Assessor asked as he poked his head into the mayor's office.

"Can you believe it, Alice quit!"

"She quit!! Wow! Good for her!"

"What did you say?"

"Oh, that's too bad. What are you going to do now without a secretary? She did a great job keeping things going smoothly here, Mayor. I think you should have given her a raise. Maybe that would have kept her here, the Assessor said with a smirk as he turned and left the mayor's office to spread the word.

Mayor Cramston got on the phone and called his wife. "Catalina, can you come in here. I need your help in running the office."

"What for, Ben? You have Alice."

"No, I don't have her. She quit!"

"Good for her!"

"What did you say, Catalina?"

"You heard me! It's about time she left. You have never treated her fairly. Shame on you! I will not come in to help you. You apologize to her immediately and stop being such a buffoon."

Mayor Cramston sputtered and said, "Wait…wait a minute, Catalina. I need you!" But his wife had hung up leaving him even more frustrated.

***

Alice was pulling up to the curb in front of the renovated storefront that was looking fantastic. "Wow!" she said out loud. "That looks great! Maybe I can get a job helping here. Who needs the mayor!"

She parked her car and headed over to see the woman who was standing outside the store looking her way.

Branyrd met Alice half-way and said, "Hi, what can I do for you?"

"Hi. I'm Alice. I used to work for the mayor. You are Branyrd, the one who came to my office, who has been mentioned in the paper as a 'wonder of a woman helping the homeless.'

"Yes, I am. I remember you from the mayor's office. That is funny! Is that what the newspapers said?" Branyrd laughed out loud.

"Yes, they said a lot of nice things about what you are doing here."

"Nice to meet you officially, Alice. You work for Mayor Cramston?"

"Yes, until a few minutes ago, that is. I quit my job. I couldn't take his attitude toward everything and everybody. He is nothing but a buffoon! Of course, I could say something worse but I am a lady and won't go there."

"Happy to hear that, Alice. But I know how he can be. I have met with him a couple of times. He put a stop to our donations from the public here. That was money we used to do the renovations."

"Hmm, I see, Branyrd. I just might be able to help you with that. I can go around and get donations by saying the mayor would love to see the homeless taken care of and would remember everyone's kindness and generosity," Alice giggled, knowing she would be fibbing just a little.

"Oh no, Alice. You could get into trouble without the mayor's consent."

"No, I don't think so. The mayor is hurting now without me. He can't do anything without my help. He will be lost and do anything I ask if he needs me back that badly."

"Well, as long as you don't get into any trouble with this, Alice. Do you really want your job back if you were unhappy working for him?"

"I know; I'm not getting any younger. I don't know if I really want to go back to work for him. I have to think about that. But this could work and it's no trouble at all, Branyrd. It's the least I can do. You have made quite a difference already in this city. Look at the area! It's been cleaned up of all the detritus since you put in some portable bathrooms and all the homeless are now looking better, healthier and cleaner too. It even smells cleaner here now. I always avoided coming here like everyone else because of the filth and degradation of the area. It is marvelous to see the improvements. Thank you, Branyrd."

"I am doing all I can to complete this mission and make a difference in the lives of all the homeless. Someone has to help them and it might as well be me."

"Well, you really are a saint, Branyrd, to take on this task or mission as you say. Congratulations on your success so far. I'm sure you will complete it all."

"Thank you, Alice. But with the help of good people like yourself, the Marines, store owners, and the homeless people who want to live better lives, I will be successful. I couldn't do it alone."

"I don't know about that, Branyrd. You appear to be a formidable young woman who knows her mind and takes on the toughest of tasks without a blink of an eye."

"Ha-ha, that is funny. If you only knew me a little while ago. I didn't know what to do and was afraid of everything. I guess I am learning to be braver and more determined."

"It was nice to meet you, Branyrd. I will see what I can do with the donations. Okay? I'll be back later to let you know how my drive worked."

"Thank you, Alice. It was a pleasure to meet you and get you on board for the homeless. They are grateful and so am I."

Alice waved goodbye as she drove away heading back to the office to meet with the mayor. She had a few choice words to say to him and wouldn't take no for an answer.

When she arrived at the office she went right in and didn't knock on the mayor's door. She told him, "Listen up and listen up good, Mr. Mayor! I have some important words and some not so nice words to share with you about what is happening in the city with the homeless and that woman, Branyrd. You will not interrupt me until I have had my say. Do you understand?"

Mayor Cramston stared at his former secretary and nodded.

CHAPTER TWENTY-ONE

Branyrd looked around at the sidewalks and street and noticed as Alice did that it was cleaner and smelled better due to the portable bathrooms. Branyrd had provided clothes for the homeless and showers in the new building. Until then she had kept working through all the smells and filth without a thought, but now it was better. She sighed and smiled upward to Heaven. "Yes, I think it is all better now, LORD. Thank you for your help. I am not finished yet, but I'm getting there. Stay with me, LORD. I need you!"

"I am always with you, Branyrd. Good work! I'm proud of you, Angel!"

"Thank you, LORD! I...I..."

"Remember, time is getting tighter now. You must complete your mission soon, Branyrd."

"Oh no, how much time do I have, LORD?" Branyrd asked in a shaky voice.

"Benedicto will be by to discuss the time factor with you soon. Just keep working away until it is done."

"Yes, LORD. I will do my best. I promise!" Branyrd sighed heavily and looked around for her Guardian Angel who was never there.

"Are you looking for me, Branyrd?" Benedicto appeared in front of her, making her jump back in alarm.

"I...I didn't see you, Benedicto. Why do you always do that to me? I could die of a heart attack if I were human."

"Yes, I bet you could, Angel, but you are not a human. I think you keep forgetting that fact."

"I look and feel human while I am here on Earth. It is hard to think of myself as an Angel while I am here. Especially since I am trying to do everything without powers."

"Yes, I noticed you have not been using yours much. That is commendable, Angel. HE is proud of you and so am I."

"Thank you, Benedicto, but there is much more to do and HE said there is little time left. How much time do I have?"

"Well, I don't think you have to worry yet. I think you are doing well with the timeline. Keep working and moving things forward any way you can."

"But I don't know the timeline, Benedicto. How do I know I am on time?" Branyrd felt exasperated once again with her Guardian Angel who was no longer standing in front or behind her.

Branyrd shook her head and mumbled some words that should not be spoken out loud, but she knew HE had heard them just the same. "Sorry, LORD!" she zipped her lips and looked Heavenward.

She was so busy looking up she didn't see the crowd forming on the street in front of the renovated store.

"Hello. I'm Branyrd. What can I do for you?"

The crowd opened and Alice stepped forward. "Hi Branyrd. These are some of my co-workers in the mayor's building. They have come to donate what they can to help the cause for the homeless.

Branyrd's eyes opened wide and so did her mouth. She was speechless. "Wow, that is so kind of all of you," she said as she watched them fill an empty bucket that was left on the sidewalk from previous donations.

As each person dropped in bills, she thanked them over and over again as they bowed to her and left. After everyone had donated and disappeared as quickly, Alice picked up the bucket now overflowing and handed it to Branyrd. "Here you go. This should help with more renovations."

"Yes, dear LORD. Yes, it will help. But now we have to see if we can buy another store to begin renovating once again," Branyrd's voice choked with tears.

"Oh, please don't cry, Branyrd. This is a happy time and only the beginning. I sent out an email to neighboring town offices about what you are doing. There will be more of this from them soon, I would imagine. All areas are having the same problem as we are with the homeless. If you can fix it, so can they if they follow your plan."

"Oh, yes, I'm sure they can. I will be here for a little while longer to do all I can to help them."

"Only for a little while longer, Branyrd? Where are you going? I thought you were staying here."

"I'm sorry, I have other missions to complete and must move on. HE wants me in other places to help those in need."

"Who is HE?" Alice asked as her brows furrowed causing lines to deepen.

"HE who watches over all of us. Do you believe in the LORD, Alice?"

"I...I guess so. It's been a while since I went to church or prayed though."

"Well, that doesn't mean you are not a good person or one who believes in HIM."

"Okay. I guess I am a good person. I try to be."

"What you did just now, Alice, constitutes a good person and will surely earn you a place one day. HE watches you as HE does all of us."

"I...I...okay. I will try to be good all the time since HE is watching me. Is HE watching me now?"

"All the time, Alice. HE watches us all the time. HE never misses a thing."

"Oh, that means he heard me swear at my boss and..."

"Yes. Did Mayor Cramston give you a hard time, Alice?"

"He didn't utter a peep until I was finished lambasting him. Oh boy! I better clean up my act after what I said to him."

"Yes, like I did."

"What? You swear, Branyrd? I don't believe it!"

"Well, believe it! I did and still slip sometimes when I get upset about something or someone."

"But you are so kind and giving to everyone. Look what you have done and so unselfishly too!"

"Thank you, Alice, but it is my job to do all this and to do it unselfishly. But HE does reward me with…"

"What? What does HE reward you with, Branyrd?"

"Oh, HE thanks me and praises me…"

"Well, that's good." Alice smiled and said, "I better get going. I need to get back to the office. I have my job back and from now on it's going to be different. Mayor Cramston has agreed to all my stipulations for staying, and I get a raise to boot. How do you like that? Evidently the rest of the people in the building told him I deserve a raise. I didn't even think they liked me. Ha!"

"Good for you, Alice. Talk about a formidable woman!" Branyrd laughed along with Alice and gave her a huge hug in thanks.

"This is only the beginning, Branyrd. We women will rule!"

"Bye, Alice. Take care and thanks again!"

CHAPTER TWENTY-TWO

Donations kept coming in daily. Alice even set up a bank account to accept everything in a safe place for Branyrd and put it in Branyrd's and Lucas's names at the Angel's request. Alice was at the bank and realized that she didn't know Branyrd's last name for the account. She called Branyrd and asked her.

"Branyrd, I'm sorry to bother you, but I need to know your last name to set up the account."

"Oh, right. I forgot about that. My last name is…" Branyrd prayed for guidance to the LORD. "What do I use for a last name, LORD?"

"You can use Angelos. It is very close to what you are, Angel," HE tittered and faded away.

"Thank you, LORD," Branyrd sighed and returned to Alice who was still waiting for her answer.

"Oh, sorry, Alice, I must have been daydreaming. My last name is Angelos."

"Thank you. That is very apropos for you, Branyrd, who is as close to angelic as it gets," Alice laughed and hung up.

Branyrd looked up and sighed again.

Alice finished up this business, went back to work, and concentrated on keeping the mayor in line and away from the street saying that she was taking care of everything.

***

There were tens of thousands in the account now and it kept growing. Branyrd felt secure she may have enough to put down a deposit on another store or to hold it until she could buy it outright.

Lucas came home each day from work with more donations that kept dribbling into the store and neighboring stores who dropped off the money to Amy to keep for Lucas. Amy and Lucas were getting closer each day and he often spoke about his boss fondly to Branyrd as they discussed the plans for the other stores.

"Amy is such a nice young woman, Lucas. Have you asked her out yet?" Branyrd dared to ask him.

"Umm, no. I didn't know if she would want to go out with me. I am, after all, still married or estranged to be exact."

"Yes, you are. But your wife has been gone for nearly two years now, Lucas. She has never contacted you about Ezra either?"

"No, she hasn't. I wondered why in the beginning but after speaking with her neighbor, Ruby, I know why. Unfortunately, we both don't have any other family to turn to in times like this."

Branyrd waited for an explanation as she wore a puzzled expression on her face. "I'm sorry to hear that about your family. What do you mean, Lucas?"

"Kiley is an alcoholic. She began drinking while I was away. Luckily, she had Ruby, a kind and caring next-door neighbor who took care of Ezra whenever Kiley went on a drinking binge. Thank God for that. Who knows what would have happened to my little guy if she had left him all alone…"

Branyrd patted Lucas on the back when he choked up. "Maybe she will come back in good time and explain herself to you and make amends."

"I don't know if I want her back, but Ezra does. He is too young to understand what she has done and I can't tell him his mother is a drunk."

"What is a drunk, Daddy?" Ezra asked as he came closer to his father and Branyrd after overhearing their conversation.

"Oh, Ezra. I didn't know you were there. Sorry, buddy. It's nothing to concern you right now. One day I will explain what I mean."

"Does that mean Mommy won't be coming home?" Ezra asked as his eyes filled.

"Well, I don't know about that, Ezra. I'm sorry. One day Mommy may come home and tell you why she left. But not right now. Okay?"

"No, I want Mommy to come home now!" Ezra cried out and ran into one of the homeless tents to get away from his father.

"I better go talk to him, Branyrd. We can talk later. Okay?"

"Sure. Take care of him, Lucas. He needs you. Maybe it's time to explain what you think he can understand so he won't keep asking about his mother."

"Maybe you're right, Branyrd," Lucas said as he hurried off to find his son.

Branyrd went to see the Marines who were looking over the other storefronts for what needed to be done. They were ready to begin on them as soon as Branyrd gave the word.

"Hi Nick. Looks like you and your buddies have finished all the beds. They look fantastic! You put eight beds in there. There's still plenty of space for more, if needed. Wow! You did an incredible job of fitting everything in. Your woodworking skills are outstanding, Nick! You should be in the business full time, but not before you finish up here," Branyrd giggled.

"Oh, you come first, Branyrd. Don't worry about that!

"Aww thanks, Nick! You are a lifesaver. I wouldn't have known what to do without your help!"

"I think the one who is the lifesaver and Angel is you! Look what you have accomplished since you came here. You have saved so many lives in the process. Thank you! You have even given me a new lease on life and those of my fellow Marines. They are going into business with me. It turns out they are all enjoying woodworking so much that they want to continue."

"It's kind of you to say. That's fabulous, Nick! You will all be a success, for sure."

"We hope so, at least we will have something to do that we all enjoy doing together. It gives us a purpose we did not have before, thanks to you."

"Enough of that, Nick. You can take all the credit, for it is you and your fellow Marines who are using the talents HE has given you to the full extent. Good for you!"

"When you say HE, Branyrd. Do you mean…?" Nick asked pointing up to Heaven.

"Yes, that is correct, Nick. HE is watching over all of you and I'm sure HE is pleased with what HE sees you have accomplished. HE brought you here to help me and the homeless. I should be thanking you."

"Oh, I…I don't know what to say. I guess I better get to work and see what my guys are doing. I don't want them to slack off. See you later, Branyrd. If you need me to do anything else, please let me know."

"Okay, Nick. I certainly will," Branyrd giggled.

***

Lucas ducked his head into the tent to get his son. Ezra was sitting on the floor of the homeless woman, Gloria's tent. She was hugging Ezra as he cried.

"I'm sorry, Gloria, he bothered you."

"Are you kidding, Lucas. It isn't every day I get to hug a handsome little boy like Ezra," she said as she patted the boy's back and rubbed circles there to calm him. "I am like his grandmother. I don't have any grandchildren of my own."

Eza looked up when Gloria stopped rubbing his back and he heard what she said. "You don't have any grandchildren, Gloria?"

"No, I don't. I have a daughter but I never see her. I don't even know where she lives."

"You can be my grandmother, since I don't have one of my own either," Ezra wiped his eyes on his sleeve and gave Gloria a hug. "Can I call you Grammy?"

Gloria was too astounded by Ezra's kind words that she choked up and couldn't talk. She turned her face away as tears threatened to fall.

"Can I, Grammy?" Ezra hugged Gloria extra tight as he waited for her response.

"Oh my! Of course, you can, Ezra. You can be my adopted grandson. How about that?"

Lucas smiled at the duo and wiped his own tears as he watched them hug.

Ezra got up and pulled Gloria up with him. "Let's go outside, Grammy. I want to tell everyone you are now my grandmother!"

"Ezra, give Gl…Grammy a minute to catch her breath."

"She is fine, Daddy. I don't care if my mommy comes back or not, now that I have a grandmother."

Gloria followed Ezra out of her tent and smiled and shrugged her shoulders at Lucas as her tears kept flowing.

"Thank you, Gloria. He needed this. Sorry, but I think you are stuck with him. Don't let him tire you out. Okay?" Lucas stated with a sigh of relief.

"No problem. It will be a good tired to be loved and needed," Gloria exclaimed with a happy sigh.

Lucas watched his son go from tent to tent as he exclaimed loud enough for all to hear as he introduced Gloria as his newfound grandmother. Lucas laughed out loud as he saw the puzzled expressions on all the faces of his fellow homeless.

Harold spouted in a rather stern tone, "If Gloria is your grandmother, then I want to be your grandfather. I'm old enough but maybe not as old as Gloria," he chuckled as he noticed the frown on Gloria's face when she looked at him.

"Really? You want to be my grandfather, Harold?"

"Yup, that's what I said, didn't I. Are you deaf or something?"

"Okay, I will call you Grandpa. Okay?"

"Sounds good to me, Ezra," Harold retorted with a wide smile and eyes that brimmed.

Fred looked sad as he watched the exchange. "Can I get into the act too? I want to be an honorary grandfather too."

"Okay, you can be my second grandfather but I have to call you by a different name. I know! I can call you Papa." Ezra jumped up and down in joy as he took his newfound grandparents and pulled them into a circle around and around.

Lucas watched in awe how one little boy could bring so much happiness to these people who had nothing. He was proud of his son and announced, "Well, I guess my family keeps growing. Welcome, Grammy, Grandpa and Papa!" He felt relieved he didn't have to explain about his wife's behavior to his son yet.

Everyone cheered as Ezra hugged his grandparents in turn looking quite pleased with himself.

Branyrd came over to see what all the excitement was about. "Well, everyone looks especially happy today."

"Yes, I have one grandmother and two grandfathers, Branyrd. Would you like to be my aunt? You can join our family too."

"I would be honored to be called Aunt Branyrd, Ezra. I've never been an aunt before."

"Okay, Aunt Branyrd. You are now part of my family." Ezra gave Branyrd a celebratory hug to induct her into his new family.

Lucas smiled and shrugged his shoulders at Branyrd and said, "That's my son. We are now one big happy family."

As they were celebrating a large car came to a halt in front of where they were all standing.

CHAPTER TWENTY-THREE

"Who is in charge here?" A tall, middle-aged and fit man asked, as he stepped out of the car wearing an expensive-looking dark suit and hat. He tipped his hat and waited for a response.

Branyrd came forward and said, "I guess I am. My name is Branyrd. How can I help you, sir?"

"Are you the one who is doing all this?" he waved his hand around the area.

"Well yes, with the help of all these people you see here."

"Hmm. Who gave you the authority to do this?"

"I have the approval of the mayor's office, sir, and we have a permit from the city. Who are you, may I ask?"

"I own one of the stores here. Are you willing to pay for my store?"

"Well, I will when I have enough funds to do that. We are a little short at the moment but I hope that will change soon."

"I spoke to Poster recently and he told me he gave you his store outright. Are you expecting another handout?"

"Oh no, sir. I would never ask you to do that unless you suggested that yourself."

"What? Do you think I would suggest that I give you my store without paying for it?"

"No. I didn't say that. Whatever you wish to do, sir. It is all up to you."

"Hmm. You are one confusing little lady. I have had this store for a few years now and no one has shown any interest in it."

"Did I speak with you? I called all the owners. I don't know your name, sir."

"Yes, I spoke with you for only a few minutes. I thought you were trying to scam me. I hung up on you. I'm sorry about that. Now I've met you, I can see you are not a scam artist."

"No, sir. I am not."

"I have to apologize again for not introducing myself to you. My name is Laurence Jonas. I bought this store from Mr. Poster. It once flourished until these…"

"Oh, I see. Nice to meet you, Mr. Jonas," Branyrd shook his outstretched hand and dismissed what she suspected he was going to say next.

"Laurence. Call me Laurence. My father is Mr. Jonas."

"Okay, Laurence. Did you come over here to see what we have been doing with the store that Mr. Poster gave us?"

"Yes, I am curious to see what you are doing and how you plan to convert this…this place into something better."

"Come this way, Laurence. Let me introduce you to the people in charge of planning and building this new community."

Lucas and Nick watched Branyrd come toward them with a tall man who they did not know. They exchanged wary glances with each other before Branyrd began introductions.

"Lucas, Nick, this is Laurence Jonas." Hands were shaken and heads nodded as Branyrd continued, "Lucas, please bring Laurence into the clinic and show him around. He owns the store next door and wanted to see what we have done so far. Nick, tell Laurence what you have done building the beds, shelves, showers, etc."

The three men went into the clinic while Branyrd watched from outside. She was pleased to see Laurence was interested and smiled as he ran his hands over the shelves, desks and beds.

After several minutes the three men came out of the clinic, shook hands once again as Laurence came over to Branyrd and the other two went back inside the clinic.

"Well, that is quite a transformation, Branyrd. These men are talented in planning and building. The carpentry work is outstanding. I could use a carpenter like that to do some remodeling in my house and office."

"As a matter of fact, Nick is the talented carpenter and Lucas is the planner. They worked together to map this clinic out."

"They are a wonder, that's for sure. I would like to discuss more about my store with you, Branyrd. Should I be going to Lucas?"

"Well, you could. He will be in charge completely when I leave."

"Leave? You are just getting started here, Branyrd."

"I know, but I have other things I must do. I will leave this all in the hands of capable Lucas and Nick. They will be able to handle anything that comes their way. In the meantime, Laurence, what do you want to discuss with me?"

"Well, I was thinking, since my store is falling into ruin and is not worth anything, I want to give…gift it to you for your noble cause. It is a commendable thing you are doing to help these people. I wish I could do more. Will you accept my store?"

"Of course, Laurence. Thank you so much for your kindness and generosity. I don't know what else to say."

"Seeing your smile and those of all the people around here is enough. You have made a difference in so many lives by doing this. I want to do whatever I can to help you."

"I appreciate all the help I can get, Laurence," Branyrd smiled wider.

"In fact, I will speak to the other owners here and get them to come on board. It would be a tax write-off for them anyway. If they don't agree, I will shame them into giving up their stores. Can I invite them down here to see what you have done so far?"

"By all means, that is a great idea, Laurence. If they see what we have done it may push them to join us in this endeavor."

"I know it will. I can't wait for them to see the beautiful carpentry work and the showers by Nick and his fellow Marines. He said they all took part in the work. Amazing!"

"Thank you, Laurence. I look forward to seeing you and the other store owners soon. Right?"

"Yes, most definitely. I will let you know. Do you have a number where I can reach you?"

Branyrd pulled out her phone and shared her number with Laurence before saying goodbye.

She smiled and sighed looking upward and said a silent prayer for all the good things that had come their way. *Thank you, Lord, for all your help. How much time do I have?*

When the Angel didn't get an answer, she looked around and whispered, "Benedicto, where are you?"

Her Guardian Angel appeared in front of her and smiled. "Looks like you are almost finished here, little Angel."

"Not yet, Benedicto. I have much more to do. One more of the store owners came forward on his own accord and offered his store to us. Now I can get it turned into a place for these people to sleep. All we need are the rest of the block to come to the same end and give up their stories."

"Do you think they will, Angel?" Benedicto smiled knowing full well what was going on.

"Yes, I do. Mr. Jonas is coming back with the rest of the owners to convince them to give us their stores too for a worthy cause. In fact, it would be a tax write-off for them, so Laurence stated."

"Hmm, I see. Things are coming along nicely, Angel."

"Yes, but I need to know how much time I have left to complete my mission, Benedicto."

Before Benedicto could answer a car came racing down the street and veering right onto the sidewalk where they were standing.

CHAPTER TWENTY-FOUR

Benedicto yanked Branyrd up in the air and flew her away as the car crashed into the tents and came to rest against one of the storefronts.

The Angels flew back down to see if anyone was hurt. They looked at the bent tents and scattered belongings that were once inside the tents but didn't see the occupants.

Branyrd raced from one tent to another checking to see if anyone was injured. Gloria wasn't inside what was left of her tent, nor was Fred or Harold. She looked around in confusion. "Where did everyone go?"

There was silence so deep that Branyrd could hear a pin drop. This silence didn't last long when everyone came out on the sidewalk at once and asked questions of Branyrd.

"What happened, Branyrd?" the Marines asked who had been working in the store.

"This car crashed onto the sidewalk. There is no one inside it. How did it get here?" Branyrd mused.

Lucas and Nick came over to Branyrd asking "Are you all right, Branyrd?"

"I'm fine. Where is everyone? I couldn't find Gloria, Fred or Harold or anyone else."

"Oh, I sent them on an errand a few minutes ago to take some of the trash we accumulated in the store after our carpentry work was completed to the alley."

A few minutes later Branyrd heard Gloria's unmistakable gravely voice yelling out in alarm. "What happened to my tent? Who did this?" She looked around accusingly.

"Oh, Gloria. Thank the LORD you are okay. Fred and Harold, I am so relieved you are unharmed too," Branyrd gave them all hugs.

Lucas went over to the abandoned car and looked inside. He noticed that someone had put a stick onto the gas pedal and tied it down. He pulled the stick away from the pedal and the engine stopped running.

Branyrd came over to see what Lucas was doing inside the car. "What's wrong, Lucas?"

"Look at this, Branyrd. Someone planned to cause this damage. This runaway car could have killed some of the people here."

"Yes, I see." Branyrd looked at the stick tied to the gas pedal and shook her head. "How could someone do this? Why would they do this?"

"Evidently someone doesn't like what we are doing here," Lucas said with a deep sigh.

"That doesn't make sense. We are here to help this community back on its feet. What good would come out of this?" Branyrd shook her head feeling despondent.

Nick gathered his fellow Marines and they pulled the car away from the building and back onto the road. They cleared out the broken glass and splintered wood from the door frame and siding.

Gloria was sitting on what was left of her tent. "What am I going to do now? Where will I sleep or keep my stuff?"

"Don't worry, Gloria. I will take care of this for you," Branyrd announced.

Fred and Harold helped clean up the area and try to salvage what they could of the tents.

Gloria gathered her belongings and stuffed them into a bag and walked away from the mess. She looked at Branyrd and said, "Thank you, Branyrd. But I will find a place to keep my stuff and sleep. You don't have to worry about me. I don't have much time left anyway." Tears dripped as she wiped them away with her new but used blouse and sniffled.

"No, you will not, Gloria," Branyrd said as she waved her hands around and produced a beautiful tent, larger than Gloria had ever seen before.

"Wow, is this mine, Branyrd?"

"Yes, it is yours until we can get you all inside the stores. We have a lot of work yet to do but this will keep you out of the rain and cold weather, even snow."

Gloria put her arms around Branyrd and wouldn't let go. "How can I thank you? You are an Angel, I know it! You gave me these clothes, fed me and now this. How could you do what you did without some power beyond Earth?"

"I didn't do anything, Gloria. What are you talking about?" Branyrd waved her hands over Gloria to wipe away the memories of what she had done.

She did the same for the others who were nearby after producing more tents to replace the damaged ones for them to sleep in.

Gloria looked inside her tent and exclaimed, "This is like a house! I can't believe it! Where did it come from? Who brought it here?"

Others were shouting out similar remarks at their new tents.

Branyrd smiled and walked around to admire the new sleeping quarters, taking no credit for any of it.

***

Lucas had seen what Branyrd had done and was far enough away from her when she waved her hands over the others. He didn't understand any of this but he knew Branyrd was not from around here. She had powers that were unexplainable.

Ezra was being kept busy inside luckily so he did not see what happened with the accident or what Branyrd had done with the tents. It would be too difficult to explain everything that had been taking place since this woman came here.

Lucas was beginning to believe in the LORD once again. How else could he explain why he had just sent the homeless, who were situated in the exact spot where the car had crashed, to the alley way to dump the trash. He could have done that himself or even some of the Marines who had offered to do it earlier.

Lucas's mind wandered as he observed the homeless having a phenomenal time inspecting their new quarters. He felt uplifted and happy for the first time in a long time. This woman who was a wonder had done this for him and for all the homeless. There was hope on the horizon and a new chance for all of them to live better lives.

He came out of his reverie when he heard a familiar sweet voice. "Lucas? What happened here?" She had seen some of the mess from a distance and then the destroyed tents had disappeared and been replaced by new, larger tents.

"Oh, hi, Amy. There was a runaway car that crashed into the building. Fortunately, no one was injured. There was no one in the car either. We still don't know how or why this happened and who is responsible."

"This is awful! Why would someone do something like this? They could have injured or killed some of the occupants of these tents."

"I know. We need to get to the bottom of this. I'll call the police to let them know what happened here. They may not come down though. They don't usually respond to problems here."

"Why wouldn't they?"

"Well, for one thing, we don't pay taxes since we don't work. They figure why should they come here to help us if we don't try to help ourselves."

"I don't believe that, Lucas." Amy was disconcerted by this and shook her head in disagreement. "No, we cannot let them get away with that. The police must come here and file a report."

"I agree, Amy. But what can we do if they don't come?"

"Then we go to the mayor and demand something be done to protect the people on the street."

"I agree with you, Amy. I don't want to argue with you but we have to be realistic about it. Most of the city doesn't want anything to do with the homeless. They want us to disappear. They consider us a blight on their neighborhood."

"I know, I have heard that from other businesses in the city. But I think they are changing their minds about this now since Branyrd has taken the reins and changed things drastically."

"Maybe. But there are still some who do not believe it will change things. They suspect we will go right back to our slovenly ways once Branyrd leaves."

"Branyrd is leaving? Where is she going?"

"I don't know. She is evasive about it. She says she has other missions to complete after this one."

"Missions? What does she mean missions? Is she a missionary from the church or some cult?"

"No, I don't think so. I think she answers to a higher power."

"Higher power? What do you mean, Lucas?"

"Do you believe in GOD? Do you believe there is something greater than we are?"

"Yes, I guess so. I don't go to church any more but do believe in GOD. It is difficult though at times to believe when I see what is happening here. There are more homeless every year and no one wanted to do something about helping them until Branyrd came along."

"Exactly! She came from beyond here. You may not want to believe this but my son believes. He told me he prayed to GOD to send down an Angel to help us."

"Ezra said that? He is so adorable, Lucas. If he believes then I guess I have to believe when this is what transpired from his prayers." Amy looked around and met Branyrd's eyes. She smiled back at her.

"I think Branyrd knows what we are talking about. She just looked our way and smiled. Maybe she really is an Angel, Lucas. How lucky we are to be deserving of HIS help."

"Yes, we are fortunate, Amy."

"Is there anything I can do to help, Lucas?"

"Yes, you can go out to dinner with me on Saturday. I get paid on Friday and want to wine and dine you."

"Okay. Don't spend all your money though on me. I know a special place to go and Ezra can come too."

"Really?"

"Be at my house at 6:00. We don't want Ezra to eat too late. I will cook something special for you both. Here's my address. See you at 6:00 on Saturday."

"We'll see you then, Amy. We look forward to it."

"Don't forget to call the police, Lucas."

"I will do that right now, Amy." Lucas couldn't stop smiling as he watched Amy walk away. He quickly dialed the police and waited to relay the information.

CHAPTER TWENTY-FIVE

The next morning Branyrd received a call from Laurence Jonas. "Branyrd, I have all the store owners at my office. They are ready to come there to see what you have done. Is this a good time?"

"Umm, can we make it in an hour or so?"

"Sure. Is everything all right?"

"Yes. We are busy at the moment but we will see you in an hour, Laurence. Thank you for getting them all together."

"No problem, Branyrd. See you then."

The police waited for Branyrd to get off the phone to continue their investigation about the car accident. They inspected the car and the damage to the building and asked questions of all who were there.

"Did you see the driver of the vehicle?" the police officer queried.

"No, there was no one driving. As you can see in the car there is a stick that was tied to the gas pedal."

The officer nodded and wrote down some more notes. "Were there any injuries?"

"No, fortunately, no one was in the tents when it came onto the sidewalk," Branyrd relayed.

"It doesn't look like the tents were damaged. How did the car get back to the street?"

"Well, we needed to get it off the sidewalk and clear out the damaged tents," Branyrd replied.

"Who moved it?" the officer asked with a furrowed brow.

"The Marines who were working on the store next door. They moved it back to the street."

"You should not have touched the crime scene here. How will we know what happened otherwise?"

"Sorry, officer. We didn't realize that at the time," Branyrd said in a somber tone.

"As far as we can see there were no injuries or damage. So, there was no crime committed here."

"Wait, officer. What about the damage to the storefront?" Branyrd asked in dismay, "What about the car? What do we do with the car?"

"Have it towed. If the owner comes looking for the car, tell him or her where you had it towed. Have the owner pay for any damage to the building."

"But…we…"

"Good day, Miss." The officers left the scene and without looking back.

Lucas came over to see what the police had said to Branyrd. "Where are they going? Are they finished with their report already?"

"I guess so. As far as they are concerned there was no accident since we had moved the car and did away with the tents and damaged goods."

"Oh boy! I didn't think of that. Sorry, Branyrd."

"I didn't know that either, Lucas. It's not your fault. I think they didn't want to help us anyway. I got the feeling they couldn't get away fast enough, which I don't understand."

"I was afraid of this, Branyrd. The police never come down here. I was surprised to see them make an effort to come this time. Well, I guess we will have to get rid of the car on our own then and forget about everything. Thank GOD no one was hurt."

"Yes, we can thank HIM for that. The officer told me to have the car towed and if the owners come looking for it, to tell them where to find it," Branyrd said.

"Wow, that was something. If someone does come looking for the car, we won't tell him/her where it is," Lucas snickered.

"I see what you mean. But what if that person wasn't the one to drive it this way?"

"Well, we will deal with that when the time comes, Branyrd. Don't worry about it. Okay? I will take care of it."

"Lucas, I don't want you to do anything. Okay? I have a friend who can help us with the car."

"A friend who can help us? Do you mean the big guy who appears around here from time to time?"

"Yes, Benedicto. He can take care of the car. He may be able to find out who the owner is too."

"Okay, if you want to handle that. I'll go check on my son. He may be driving the guys inside the store crazy as they stain the furniture."

Benedicto appeared shortly thereafter hearing his name and took care of the car. He said, "I'll see what I can do about finding the owner."

"Thanks, Benedicto. I'm not even going to ask about how you plan to do that."

Benedicto did the quirky thing with his eyebrow and disappeared along with the car but checking first to make sure to cloak himself and the vehicle away from prying eyes.

***

An hour later, several cars drove up and stopped in front of the stores. The first person who came forward was

164

Laurence Jonas. He extended his hand to Branyrd and waited for the rest of the contingent to come closer for introductions.

Laurence introduced all the men and women who were owners of the rest of the block of stores. He had filled them in on what Branyrd was doing but turned to her to tell them more about her plans.

Branyrd smiled at everyone and said, "It's a pleasure to meet all of you. Thank you for coming today. Let's go to the clinic which is almost completed. The Marines who are working there are finishing up the staining of the woodworking they created."

Everyone filed into the store which was large enough to hold them all. They looked around and were in awe at what had been done so far.

Laurence pointed out the workmanship of the desks, shelves and beds to the store owners. "Can you believe the craftsmanship of this work? These Marines are certainly talented craftsmen."

"I would love to have one of these desks in my office and one in my home too," one man said.

"The workmanship is beautiful. Everything is well-made and attractive too," a woman expressed with admiration.

Turning to Branyrd, one store owner asked, "Where did you find these craftsmen? I have been looking for someone to do some work in my home for a long time."

Branyrd didn't answer but called out to Nick who was the lead carpenter, "Come over here. There are some people who would like to meet you."

Nick stopped what he was doing and looked up in surprise.

"Thank you, Nick. Sorry to bother you. These people are store owners on this block. They are interested in the work you and your fellow Marines have done here."

After introductions and handshakes all around, one man asked, "Where did you train to create such beautiful woodwork?"

"Thank you for your kind words. My father was a carpenter all his life and taught me from a young age. I have been doing this ever since."

"You are quite talented, Nick. Do you have a business somewhere? I would be interested in having you do some work for me in my home and for my office."

"Well, I am only beginning. I have not found a place to work yet. After I complete everything here, I will do that."

Branyrd smiled at Nick and suggested, "Why don't you use one of these stores for your shop? There are plenty here as long as we can convince one of these owners to give up his/her store for that purpose."

Several of the owners exchanged glances before answering, "I will give you my store, Nick, if you promise to put me on the top of your list to do some work. Of course, I will pay you handsomely," one owner exclaimed.

"Thank you, sir. I appreciate that. I will think about it and get back to you." Nick turned to go after thanking everyone for their interest in his work.

"Maybe he would rather have my store," one woman said, "it's a lot bigger than yours."

"He probably has something else in mind," the man retorted.

Branyrd listened to the owners haggle back and forth about whose store was more suitable to Nick's work. She waited for them to calm down before speaking. "What have you planned for your stores?"

"We came here to see what you were doing and now we will make our decisions about what to do," another owner stated in a serious tone.

Laurence stepped forward and exclaimed loudly, "What's wrong with all of you? We discussed this before we got here. You all agreed to give up your stores to Branyrd so she could continue on with this incredible work she has done. If you don't do this our city will go back to ruin once again. You must step forward and help this wonder of a woman out. No one has been able to do what she has done."

"You are right, Laurence. Sorry about our procrastination. We all know no one will purchase these stores until there is a complete transformation."

"What are you talking about? Branyrd is not going to do the work and have you turn on her and sell your places. Are you all crazy? The purpose of this is to have a place for the homeless to live and work. Isn't that correct, Branyrd?"

"Yes, you are correct, Laurence. I am doing this mainly for them to get out of the cold weather and have a purpose. They will have jobs to do to keep up this neighborhood once I am gone. It will be run by Lucas with Nick's help to complete the renovations."

"How can you guarantee the homeless won't come back as before and destroy our city?" one angry owner inquired.

"I can't guarantee you anything, sir. But I can guarantee once the homeless have a safe place to stay, eat, gather and receive medical care, they will keep it up in good shape. I have spoken with all the homeless here. They are excited about this new life they will have which will enable them to live better, healthier, safer and allow them to regain their dignity which has been sadly lacking."

"See, this is a worthwhile project for us all. Now get out your paperwork and sign over your stores to this woman once and for all. There has been enough talk, action is what we need now. You know as well as I these stores will go to ruin if we don't do something. Now is your chance to make a difference in our city," Laurence stated in a firm manner as he gave each owner a steely gaze.

Heads nodded and papers were shuffled as their lawyers collected the paperwork and signed it all over to Branyrd.

Branyrd signed where they instructed her and collected the paperwork. Lucas came over when Branyrd waved at him to sign next to her name on all sheets.

"We are all set now, Branyrd. Do you have a lawyer to take care of this for you?" Laurence asked.

"No, but I know someone who can help get this all together for me. I can't thank you all enough for your kindness and generosity to help us build a safe place for these people to live."

Branyrd announced in a loud voice to all the homeless, "We are going full-speed ahead with our project! You will soon have a new place to sleep, eat and receive care."

Exclamations could be heard as her words traveled throughout the tent city. Soon there was a line of people there to thank Branyrd and the former owners. Hands were shaken and backs were patted in thanks.

Nick and the Marines came out of the store where they were completing the staining of the furniture to see what was going on.

"We have them all, Nick!" Branyrd announced in jubilation. "You can get started on the other stores now."

"That's the best news I've heard in a long time," Nick said with a broad smile. He motioned to his fellow Marines, "Let's go, guys. We need to pick up some more materials at the hardware store so we can get started on the other stores. Cam also has donated some supplies that he is keeping at his construction business. He said we can pick them up any time we need them."

Branyrd handed Nick some money to take care of the purchases and said, "Thank Cam for me for the donations."

"Will do, Branyrd," Lucas replied before joining the others.

Branyrd turned around and walked the former owners back to their cars with her last words of gratitude.

"Laurence, I don't know how you did it, but I am forever grateful to you as are the homeless here as well. They are quite excited to see the results and now are able to use the facilities, thanks to you."

"My pleasure, Branyrd. You are the one who should be thanked for what you have been able to do here. Who knows what would have happened to our city if you hadn't stepped in to make a difference."

"It's not me, Laurence. I am working for a greater power. HE is the one who should be thanked."

"Hmm, I see, Branyrd. So, you are saying that this greater power has empowered you to perform miracles here?"

"Well, I guess you could say that," Branyrd tittered.

"Whatever and whoever sent you here and empowered you to do this, I thank them," Laurence stated with a smile and a nod as he escorted the rest of the group to their cars. He waved a last goodbye to Branyrd as they all drove away.

There was someone who watched the contingent drive away who had an agenda of his own.

CHAPTER TWENTY-SIX

The watcher got into his car and headed to the mayor's office. He had plans of his own about the homeless community.

Mayor Cramston was in his office mumbling over some new business that wasn't working out. He yelled out to Alice, his secretary, to come in to his office. When she didn't answer after the last call, he reluctantly picked up the phone and used the intercom to reach her.

"Alice, please come in here right away. I need you to take a letter."

Alice waited a few seconds and then answered, "Yes. I will be there shortly." She sat for another couple of minutes.

There was no way she was going to give him the upper hand in anything from now on. She had told him that she would not answer if he did not call her through the intercom. There would be no more yelling from his office to hers. She was going to stand her ground or else she would quit again. She giggled to herself before getting up from her desk with her pad and pen in hand to see what the buffoon wanted now.

Before she could open the mayor's door a man rushed into her office and stopped beside her. He was sweating and looked disheveled as if he had been on the losing end of a fight. He had dark hair that stood out all over and his eyes were dark and menacing. She didn't stare too long for fear of being drawn into a dark place.

"Can I help you, sir?" Alice stammered clearly unsettled.

"No, I need to see the mayor. Get out of my way." He opened the mayor's door without knocking. He slammed it behind himself and started yelling at the top of his lungs.

"Do you know what is happening here, Mayor Cramston? Our community is being taken over by the homeless and that woman!"

"Calm down, Alfred. We don't need the whole city to hear you. Sit down. We need to discuss this further," the mayor said in a tense voice.

Alice was outside her boss's door and listening to what they were saying. She couldn't believe the mayor was plotting something so dastardly. She had to do something to stop him.

She hurried back to her desk and picked up the phone. She had Branyrd's number on her connections and dialed it quickly.

"Branyrd? This is Alice. You will not believe what I heard! We need to put our heads together to stop the mayor."

"Hi Alice, Slow down. What's going on?"

"I overheard something terrible. A man came into the mayor's office and spoke to him about what you are doing here. I listened outside the mayor's office and heard them saying something about putting the homeless out of their misery. They are planning to destroy the homeless community and all that you have done so far. Did you have an accident there recently?"

"Yes, we did have a situation with a runaway car that skipped the curb and ran into the tents and a building."

"Is everyone okay?" Alice asked in shocked.

"Yes, no injuries. Fortunately, all the occupants were elsewhere at the time," Branyrd explained.

Alice continued, "Well this man was most likely the one who crashed the car into your building recently."

"What? That's surprising. I thought the mayor was on board about what I am doing here."

"Yes, I thought so too, Branyrd. I don't understand why he would undermine what you have accomplished for the good of the city. You are not only helping the homeless but also helping the whole city get stronger and safer for all."

"Thank you, Alice, for your kind words. I will continue doing all I can. Don't worry, I will have a talk with the mayor and see what I can do to get him on our side."

"I don't think you will convince him. He has this agenda and…maybe he owes someone something. I will keep my eyes and ears open. I'll see what I can discern and get back to you."

"Okay, Alice. Please don't get yourself in trouble. Keep in touch with me and let me know that you are okay. I don't trust the mayor or this man, whoever he is, not to do something rash by the sounds of what you said."

"I agree. Don't worry about me, Branyrd. I can take care of myself, the mayor and his cronies too," Alice laughed nervously.

"Take care, Alice. I'll talk to you soon."

"No problem, Branyrd. I'll keep you up-to-date on any new developments. Keep your eyes open over there too."

"I will, Alice, Thank you. Goodbye."

"Bye for now."

Branyrd summoned her Guardian Angel to come asap, "I need you, Benedicto. Something is in the wind and I don't know if I will be able to handle it alone."

"What's the matter, Angel?" Benedicto appeared next to her looking perplexed.

Branyrd explained everything Alice had reported. "What do you think he will do, Benedicto?"

"I haven't seen anything coming yet. I will pay a visit with the mayor. You can come along. I think it is time we spoke to him and found out what he is going to do."

"Maybe I should have a talk with the LORD first. HE knows what is going to happen. HE will tell me if he wants me to know beforehand."

"You can do that, little Angel. But don't worry too much. HE will be watching over you and keeping you safe from harm."

"I'm sure HE will, Benedicto. But what about all these defenseless people all around us. They can't protect themselves. They need our help."

"They will have our help, I assure you, Branyrd. I won't leave them unprotected and neither will you. We are here to make sure they are safe at all costs."

***

Lucas, Nick and the other Marines returned with all the lumber and supplies loaded down in a truck they borrowed from Cam. He lent them the truck to pick up the donated supplies.

Branyrd watched them unload the materials and waited until they finished.

Lucas looked over at Branyrd and came her way when he saw the worried expression on her face. "Are you okay, Branyrd?"

"That is what I wanted to talk to you about, Lucas. There may be trouble coming our way. It has something to do with the car that crashed into our building recently."

"Do you know who did that? We should call the police and report that person right away."

"Well, I don't know who the person is but I got a tip about something that was heard in the mayor's office in a meeting between the mayor and an unnamed man. This person will keep me in the loop about anything else that may come up."

"Is this person Alice by any chance?" Lucas queried.

"Well, I don't want to mention any names to get anyone in trouble."

"Hmm, I see. Okay, I won't mention any names either. Do you mean the mayor was behind that accident? What is he planning to do?"

"Thank you, Lucas. It looks like it could be the mayor behind all this. This person did not know anything else. But will let me know if there is anything further to report. We need to keep on the lookout for any problems. I will keep guard tonight and have Benedicto with me for backup. No one will come near him, I'm sure, because of his size."

"I know I wouldn't try anything to get his dander up, Branyrd. He scares me even though he has been nothing but kind and helpful to all of us."

"Yes, Benedicto can be frightening if you don't know him. He is the kindest and sweetest …man you could ever hope to meet. But you do want him on your side at all times," Branyrd said with a smirk.

"Well, you should know. Since you know him better than I. But what do you suggest we do, Branyrd?"

"Why don't you make sure everything is locked down with all the supplies inside the buildings. I will check on all the homeless to ensure they are safe too. I need to make them aware of the possible dangers ahead."

"Okay, I'll get right on it. Don't worry, we are all here to help you in any way we can, Branyrd. I know my fellow Marines would never leave a lady in distress."

"Thank you, Lucas. Take care of Ezra. I will put out your box bedroom again and make sure it is filled with whatever you need."

"Will do. He is my priority always, Branyrd."

Lucas raced back to the stores to let the Marines know what was going on.

Nick came over to Branyrd and laid a hand on her shoulder, "Branyrd, we will stay the night. We have beds in there so we can keep watch from inside the clinic. We won't displace any of the homeless though who are not well and now sleeping inside since it is getting colder."

"I appreciate that but you need not worry. Benedicto and I can handle anything that comes this way."

"No, I won't stand by without helping. I know my fellow Marines feel the same way, Branyrd. Not another objection. We will be here for you."

"Thank you, Nick." Branyrd hugged him in gratitude even though she knew that she and Benedicto would do their magic to prevent any problems coming their way.

After Nick went back to report to the other Marines about what he had told Branyrd, Benedicto appeared and nodded to Branyrd. "Listen, I heard everything. You know you have me to help, Angel. I will keep an eye and an ear out for any trouble and nip it right away."

"Thank you, Benedicto. But you know we cannot do anything that would cause anyone to question who or what we are."

"Don't you think they already suspect we are not from here?" Benedicto raised his eyebrows in a quirky way to cause Branyrd to giggle out loud.

"Sorry about that, Benedicto. But you do make the funniest faces at times. I don't know how you can raise one eyebrow so high and the other stays straight. It is funny to look at."

"One of my many talents, little Angel," Benedicto answered with a smirk and another eyebrow lift.

"Okay, I get it. They already know we are different. But they do not know how different yet. I was told by HIM not to cause any disruptions or announcements that we are not who we appear to be."

"Yes, I got the memo too, Branyrd. HE told me in strong terms that we must be careful," Benedicto raised his brow at Branyrd and disappeared.

The Angel looked around to make sure no one had seen the Guardian Angel do his disappearing act.

CHAPTER TWENTY-SEVEN

Branyrd kept watch all day, and dismissed the Marines to go home, eat dinner and come back later. Nick and Lucas insisted on staying close to her in case they were needed. Nick grabbed some sandwiches from a local sub shop and came back offering one to Lucas, Ezra and Branyrd.

"Thanks, Nick," Branyrd announced, "I'm not hungry. I grabbed something already. You two go sit down inside and eat. I will keep watch."

Branyrd noticed Benedicto had come back and was going in and out of the tents with bags of food for the homeless. Shouts of surprise and delight were heard all around. He came over to Branyrd after his deliveries and sat on the curb next to her with a coffee in his hand for her. Though Branyrd didn't need to eat or drink she had acquired a taste for coffee from her first mission to Earth which Benedicto remembered.

"Thank you, Benedicto. It's been a while since I had one of these."

"My pleasure, little Angel. Well, everyone is fed and soon will be asleep. I waved a hand over each tent to make sure they did fall asleep soon after eating to ensure they are not aware of what is going on outside. I expect there will be plenty of action some time tonight."

"Do you really know what is going to happen before it happens, Benedicto?" Branyrd quizzed him.

"Only what HE wants me to know. I can't predict what will happen unless HE opens my eyes to everything."

"Will HE allow me to know everything too one day?" Branyrd asked in a hesitant tone.

"Well, I guess HE could. But who knows. HE is always protective of HIS Angels. You are one very special Angel, Branyrd. HE will always keep you safe."

"I know HE will but I am curious as to what HE will allow me to do. Can I disappear at will like you, Benedicto?"

"Hmm, that I do not know. I disappear when HE calls me most of the time. But I can do that any time I want by just thinking about doing it. I bet you can do it too, Angel."

"Really? I can disappear at will like you? Let me try. What do I have to do, Benedicto?"

"I don't think this is a good idea right now, Angel. We need to stay right here and keep watch."

"Okay, but later on when it is safe, I want to disappear like you."

"We will see, Branyrd. Later on, we will see," Benedicto smiled and winked at her and was gone.

"Damn it – er, I mean darn it! Why does he keep doing that?" she sighed in exasperation.

Branyrd looked around when she heard something. She got up from her perch on the curb and followed the sound down the alleyway.

She knew the box bedroom was there; she could see the hologram of its outline ensuring Lucas and Ezra were safely inside. She moved slowly, keeping to the dark sides of the alley and looked deep into the darkness. There was something there. She could feel the evil oozing out of it or him. Now was the time for her to be able to disappear like Benedicto always did. So far, she could only disappear if he took her along with him. Where was her Guardian Angel now that she needed him? Exasperation seeped into her mind as she looked around.

***

Nick and the other Marines were snug inside the clinic along with several others who had been sleeping there instead of in their outside tents. They were the ones who needed to be watched closely since they were the sickest of them all.

Each night as the cold intensified and the snow came down heavily, more and more homeless came inside to get out of the cold. Branyrd had made sure there was heat and electricity right from the beginning for this purpose. A couple of showers also had been put in by one of the Marines who was a part-time self-professed plumber. These were in constant use by the homeless who couldn't get enough of the feel of having hot water. More would be installed soon to handle the crowd who waited in line each day and night.

The Marines had seen the need for more and more beds and had begun building more bunk beds which could be stacked two and three against the walls. The clinic was getting more crowded each night as more homeless slipped in to sleep on a vacant bed. Tomorrow they would be working on the other buildings and building extensive sleeping quarters enough for all and then some.

One Marine who had been an EMT in the service attended to the sickest after purchasing some first aid kits to keep handy. There wasn't much he could do for them. Some were infested with old bug bites which he treated right away while others had bed sores or most aptly explained, ground sores, from sleeping on the ground for so many years, and still others were weak, coughing and possibly dying from the inside out due to the inclement weather and intense cold they had been subjected to repeatedly. The homeless began to call him Doc and the name stuck.

Doc, who had a kind heart, suffered along with these people. Watching them broke his heart and he vowed he would do all he could to help them. He knew someone who could assist him and now was the time to get his help.

He tossed and turned after making sure everyone was comfortable and asleep before succumbing himself. A plan was formatting in his mind as he slept which he planned to put into place. This is the least he could do for these people.

If this little woman, Branyrd, could do all this then he could do his share being a strong, strapping young man. He sighed in his sleep and smiled.

***

Benedicto watched Branyrd creeping along the alleyway. He could see up ahead there were three men wearing dark hoodies hugging the shadows as they made their way forward. He could see Branyrd looking up from her hiding place every so often. He was concerned that she may not have detected them yet. He also knew she was struggling with how to disappear. He waited another moment before moving forward and flying over to her side to assist and also protect her as he was meant to.

He whispered to her as he came closer, "Branyrd take my hand."

"What? Where did you come from? I was hoping you were coming soon. There is someone coming this way. I can feel his darkness and evil flowing out around him. This is not good, Benedicto. What are we to do? I haven't mastered or even tried to master how to disappear like you do."

"Yes, I know that, little Angel. That is why I am here to help you. Take my hand now."

"Yes, okay. Wait a minute. Don't be so bossy!"

Benedicto guffawed and grabbed Branyrd's hand pulling her up and away.

"Where are you taking me, Benedicto?" she asked in alarm. "The man is that way."

"I know, Branyrd. But we are going to go around behind them."

"Them? What do you mean them? There are more?"

"Yes, there are three to be exact, maybe more."

"What do you think they are doing here? Are the others in danger?"

"Yes, everyone is in danger. We must stop them and do it now before it's too late." Benedicto wore a serious and intense expression on his large, handsome face, one which Branyrd had never seen before.

"What do you know, Benedicto. Please tell me! What are they going to do?"

"They have evil in their hearts, that is for certain, Branyrd. The evil they have there is to destroy everyone and everything in its path. That is why HE sent me to help you clear out this evil."

"But how can we do that? Is HE going to help us?"

"HE is here now and will help us. You know that, Branyrd. We can't do anything without HIS help."

"Yes, of course. Why do I keep forgetting? I guess being in this human body makes me think more like a human every day I am here on Earth. I must think like an Angel. Right?"

"Well, that is one way to deliberate on it, Angel. You are smarter than you give yourself credit for," Benedicto's face transformed into a beautiful smile as he looked at the Angel's sweet, little face.

Branyrd found herself blushing and blinking from the brilliant aura that was in front of her. She watched as the aura became brighter and grew to surround them and light up the alleyway revealing the three men who stopped in their tracks and covered their eyes to protect them from the brightness.

Benedicto dropped down with Branyrd beside him in front of the three startled men who dropped their guns and other items at their feet.

One man yelled out loud, "What is happening? Who are you?"

The other two were speechless and shivered and hid behind the first man.

"Who are you?" Benedicto roared loud enough to break nearby glass windows which began to crack and crumble as the glass dropped to the ground nearby.

The men turned and ran the other way and never looked back as Benedicto and Branyrd laughed long and hard and raised their hands in thanks to HIM above.

The noise of the glass cracking woke up the Marines who were alert to such things when they were in the war. They came running along the opposite end of the alley to see what was happening.

Nick and Doc arrived first and asked, "What's going on? What was that noise?"

Benedicto smiled and let Branyrd take over the explanation as he managed to disappear without anyone noticing that he was gone.

A few seconds later Lucas and Ezra appeared out of thin air to see why they were awakened and noticed everyone standing around looking at them with a quizzical expression.

"What's the matter? What happened? We heard some noise and came out to investigate."

"Came out of where?" Nick asked. "One minute you were not here and the next you appeared out of thin air. That is very strange."

"Oh, well, you will have to ask Branyrd about that," Lucas chuckled.

"Yep, ask Aunt Branyrd," Ezra smirked, feeling special because he knew a secret no one else did.

CHAPTER TWENTY-EIGHT

After explanations were finished, the Marines collected the guns and other items, some were more ammunition and others were sticks of dynamite. They disposed of these and went back to check on everyone who were now milling around and asking questions about the noise.

Branyrd spoke to all the homeless and explained, "There is no danger now; you are all safe. It's still too early to get up, go back to sleep." Everyone returned to their beds and settled down.

A few hours later Branyrd called out to Benedicto who appeared from the alleyway with bags of items for breakfast. Once the others noticed the bags and smelled the aromas of egg sandwiches, they forgot all talk of any danger earlier and hurried over to collect their early breakfast much to the relief of both Branyrd and Benedicto.

The Marines were back to work in the other stores building and refurbishing the insides and outsides. Paint cans were placed in front of each storefront as some of the homeless helped paint so that the Marines could work inside with the more difficult jobs of installing more showers, building beds, walls and other furniture to outfit each place. Even Ezra grabbed a brush and did what he could to help, working on the low areas while the others began at the top of the doors and storefronts.

Branyrd smiled as she watched everyone busily taking part in this restoration. She thought over the night's adventures and sighed in relief that nothing had happened to any of these lovely people who had become so precious to her. She felt like before on her first mission. She still missed the people she had come to cherish from then and hoped they were doing well. She would miss everyone here too, especially Lucas, Ezra, Nick, Doc, Gloria, Fred, Harold and everyone else who had been supportive of her efforts to make these changes.

She felt a tingle in her pocket from her phone. She looked at the screen and saw it was Alice. "Hi Alice. How are you?"

"Oh, Branyrd, I…think…something terrible is going to happen!"

"What? Take your time, Alice, and take a deep breath and tell me."

"I overheard the mayor talking again to that man who came here before. He had two others with him this time. They were yelling at the mayor and complaining about something. They said they went to the alley with guns and some dynamite."

"I see. I know about them, Alice. No worries. They won't come back."

"How do you know about them? I heard them talking about going there. Did you see them already?"

"Yes, they were here but Benedicto frightened them away. He is a large man and they did not want to mess with him."

"But they had guns and dynamite. They could have hurt him, you and the others too."

"I am aware of that, Alice. We handled it. They won't come back here, I assure you."

"Are you sure? Do you want me to call the police?"

"No need to do that. Nothing happened."

"But…but…what if they try something else?" Alice asked in terror.

"I…we will handle whatever comes our way. No need for you to worry. But I do appreciate you keeping me informed."

"Okay, I will keep my eyes and ears open though in case there is anything else to share. I don't want anything to happen to you…or anyone else," Alice said in a choked whisper.

"Thank you, Alice. You are a good person to have as a friend."

"Yes, I am your friend, Branyrd. Don't you forget that. I have your back."

"I believe you, Alice. I have your back too," Branyrd smiled with tears glistening in her eyes.

"Okay, well, I had better go. The mayor might get suspicious that I am spying on him. I am not the only one who is keeping a close eye on him. There are many in this building who know he is corrupt and one to watch. They all want him out of office. There are many who would be much better at the job than him."

"That is good to know, Alice. I'm sure there are many other good men in the city who could be mayor if given a chance to run."

"Yes, and I would vote for any one of them. Got to go. Talk to you soon, my friend."

"Okay, my friend, I will be here." Branyrd smiled and sighed knowing that she may not be here much longer if HE had anything to say about it. Once everything was completed, she would be pulled and sent on another mission somewhere else.

Branyrd looked around at the tents that were now dwindling down to a handful. Most of the people were inside keeping warm and had taken down their tents and belongings and stored them inside lockers the Marines had supplied for them. Each locker had their name printed in bold, bright letters exclaiming that each person had property for the first time safely stored in one place.

The Angel could see the smiles and pride returning to these no longer homeless people who now had a purpose in life for as long as they lived. The plans Lucas had formulated with Branyrd's help were coming together in a perfect way to help these poor people. She wondered if this community would continue to grow and spread to other homeless communities so they could do the same thing to keep the inhabitants in a safe and cleaner environment for all.

As she was musing over this, she heard a familiar voice calling her. She turned to see Amy, the manager of the hardware store, Safety First.

"Hi, Amy. How are you? Nice to see you again."

"Hi, Branyrd. Same here. I stopped by to see Lucas. He called in sick today. Is he okay?"

"Oh, I don't know. I haven't spoken with him today yet. Let's go see. He's inside the stores working with the other Marines."

Amy looked displeased as she heard this but didn't say anything until she saw Lucas. "Here you are, Lucas. How come you didn't come into work today? You don't look sick."

"Umm...sorry, Amy. I needed to help these guys finish up here. There is so much yet to do in order for all the homeless to have a place to stay out of the cold."

"Oh, I see. You could have told me that. I wouldn't have refused you some time off," Amy said in a disappointed tone.

"I really am sorry, Amy. You can dock me a day's pay. I deserve it!"

"No, I will not do that. But this is a warning, Lucas. Next time you need to take some time off, please let me know and I will give you as much time as you need. In fact, I will come and help you out if you need me. I am adept at woodworking and all kinds of stuff like you are doing here. My father taught me well. I was the boy he never had," Amy's voice no longer displayed the anger or hurt she had previously felt.

"Really? That would be great, Amy!" Lucas came over to her and took her into his arms giving her a huge hug in front of everyone. He stepped back with a blush to his cheeks when he realized what he had done.

Amy smiled at him and said, "You are welcome, Lucas. Anytime you need me, just call. You know where to find me."

"Yes, I do. Thanks, Amy," Lucas returned the smile and blushed some more.

Amy stopped to say goodbye to Branyrd, "Thanks, Branyrd. I will be coming around here more to help if you need me as I told Lucas. I can do anything the men can do."

"I believe you can do anything you put your mind to do, Amy. You are one surprisingly talented young woman. Lucas is fortunate to have you."

"He is?" Amy quizzed in surprise.

"Yes, I believe he is. He just doesn't realize how lucky he is. Someone may have to tell him," Branyrd winked at Amy and left her standing there with a wide smile.

"Well, it looks like you have a girlfriend, Lucas," Nick announced for all to hear.

"Oh, come on. She is my boss and a friend, Nick."

"I don't think so, Lucas. Wake up, buddy. You have it bad and so does she."

"But I'm still married."

"You haven't been married for years now. You told me she left you when you were still in the service. If she didn't come back then, she won't come back now. Come to your senses, Lucas."

"I know. I have to find her and get her to divorce me. This is a waste of time to hang onto something I haven't had in a long time. But I worry about Ezra. He needs his mother."

Ezra was listening in the other room and came in to announce, "I miss Mommy, but I like Amy better. She is nicer than Mommy. Amy listens to me and doesn't leave me alone."

"Oh, Ezra. I'm so sorry Mommy did that to you. She was sick and couldn't help it. I will find her and she will tell you that herself one day. I like Amy too, son. I like her a lot."

"Find her, Daddy, and let's get divorced so we can marry Amy!"

"Wow, out of the mouths of babes, Lucas! At least one of you is smart!" Doc announced with a titter as he came forward to add his opinion.

The other Marines nearby who were also listening cheered.

"Okay, guys. Stop ganging up on me. I know what I have to do. I will do it! Now, everyone, get back to work. Subs are on me today."

Another cheer went out from all as they went back to work with a happier and faster beat.

Doc suddenly dropped his hammer when he saw Harold limping toward him. "What's wrong, Harold? Did you fall?"

"No, I woke up like this, Doc. I found this inside my tent." He handed a stick of dynamite to the Marine.

"Where was this, Harold?" Doc asked in alarm, meeting the eyes of his fellow Marines.

"It was inside my tent. I slept outside last night because I needed some air. It was getting too hot inside for me. I went to lay down and landed on it hurting my bum hip. It hurts like the devil, Doc. Can you give me something to ease the pain?"

"Sure, Harold. Take these for the pain and lay down inside and rest. I will take care of your tent. You shouldn't be outside in this cold."

"I know but sometimes I miss being in the elements, you know what I mean, Doc. I like the fresh air. It's in my makeup to sleep outside. I have done it for too many years to recall."

"I know, Harold, but now it will be different. You will have a safe place inside to sleep, eat and be taken care of for the rest of your life. No more sleeping outside. Okay?"

"Okay, Doc. Whatever you say. I don't want to find anything like that in my bed again. Who the hell put it there anyway?" Harold asked in confusion.

"Do you know what this is, Harold?" Doc asked.

"Oh, hell, yeah! I've seen my share of dynamite! I used it when I was in the war and kicked the asses of many men on the opposite side."

"I bet you did, Harold," Doc chuckled but then got serious again. "Go lay down. I'll check on you later."

"Okay, will do. You're the doctor."

Doc smiled at that remark but left to commiserate with his fellow Marines. "What do you make of this being in his tent, guys?"

"I don't know how that got there. The men never got any further than the alley according to Branyrd. They dropped their guns and dynamite and ran away after Benedicto frightened them. I would be frightened too if he came at me in a menacing way!" one Marine exclaimed who was large and quite fit himself.

"We better keep our eyes and ears open. Someone is lurking around that we may have missed while working. Check with Branyrd and let her know what we found. Maybe she knows something. I'm going to see how Harold is doing. Thank God it didn't explode when he lay down on it," Doc announced with a deep sigh. "Of course, he would have had to light it up first. But you know Harold, you can light a fire with his tooting," Doc joked trying to de-escalate the situation.

"Ha, I know. Somebody up there likes Harold, evidently. I'll go see Branyrd and let her know," Lucas announced as he shook his head at Doc's remark and went in search for her.

Branyrd was out walking the block and checking on the homeless who were still on the street. She wanted to make sure they were okay. She had to do her magic with a few of them who were quite disturbed mentally and unable to handle what was going on around them. She calmed them down and headed back to the stores when she ran into Lucas who was looking a little disturbed himself.

"What's wrong, Lucas."

"Look what Harold found inside his tent. He slept outside last night. We thought he was inside but I guess he slipped out unnoticed and lifted the flap of his tent and crawled inside and found this."

"Oh no, how did that get there? Who would have done that? The men didn't get this far."

"I know. That's what I told the others. We put all the dynamite and guns in a barrel and took it away. The police said they would dispose of it after I told them I found it in the alley. They were coming back here to check around for any more. Should I call them again, Branyrd?"

"Maybe we should. Let them look around and make sure there isn't any more around to cause a danger to our people here."

"Hmm, they are our people, aren't they, Branyrd? I feel as if we are a community, all of us together. We are a family."

"I guess we are, Lucas. I didn't think of it that way. But I guess we are," Branyrd smiled at Lucas and patted him on the back. "Good work, young man. You have done so much since we began all this. I am proud of you."

"Thank you, Branyrd. I couldn't have done any of this without you. None of us could. You have given us a purpose in life, a better direction to take, a new lease on life that we couldn't have done without your guidance. We thank you."

"No need to thank me. I am doing what is expected of me, Lucas. I'm happy to be of help and feel needed. It has given me a purpose too."

"I'll call the police and report this. It's in their hands now. But I'll keep an eye out for anything else that may appear."

"Good idea, Lucas. You're a good man to have around. We can all depend on you. Oh, by the way, keep that girl close. She is special."

"What girl?"

"Lucas, you know who I am talking about," Branyrd tittered and walked away.

"I guess everyone is keeping tabs on me," he said in response to her back

.

CHAPTER TWENTY-NINE

The police showed up shortly thereafter and checked inside the remaining tents, the alley and its garbage barrels and inside the stores where the Marines stood aside to let them search. After the search was completed, the police questioned the men and Harold for anything further to add to their report.

One man came forward in an unsteady gait, stopping in front of the police with a stick in his hand. "Are you looking for this, Officer?"

The officer in charge stepped forward and took the stick of dynamite from the man's hand asking, "Where did you get this, sir?"

"I found it in my stuff inside my tent. It's not mine." The man turned to go back to his tent in the same swaying gait.

"Wait a minute, sir! I want to see your tent and belongings." The officer followed the man back to his sleeping quarters with two more officers close behind.

Branyrd and the others watched in shock as they exchanged wary glances amongst themselves.

"Where did he get that?" Branyrd asked anyone who could answer.

"I have no idea. That guy is not all together, you know that, right?" Lucas announced with a sad shake of his head.

"I saw him the first day I was here. He came up to me and asked if I was his sister," Branyrd shared.

"Oh, that's right, his sister hasn't come to see him in a long time. She may be dead by now. I met her once but never saw her again. She was quite upset with her brother at that time. She said she tried to help him for years to get off drugs, to no avail. I guess she finally gave up," Lucas stated with a sigh.

"Where is he getting the drugs if he has no money?" Branyrd asked in confusion.

"That's a good question. The police may find some stuff there that will put him in jail. Maybe that would be a good way for him to get sober. I've known him for a couple of years and still don't know his name. He never shared that with anyone. I was surprised to hear him speak to the police. He has no idea he could be in trouble."

"I'm going over there to see if I can help him," Branyrd said, moving in that direction quickly. She looked up to Heaven and said a silent prayer for help. She hoped Benedicto could hear her too as she whispered his name.

Benedicto whispered back, "I will be there, little Angel, and help you. Don't worry."

When she got to the man's tent the police were inside moving everything outside. One officer was holding onto the man to keep him out of the way.

"I'll stay with him, Officer," Branyrd said with a smile. Turning to the man she asked, "Are you all right? What is your name? We met the first day I was here when you asked me if I was your sister. My name is Branyrd."

The unstable man turned his rheumy eyes toward Branyrd and said, "I…I don't remember. I…think I am… He told me not to share my stuff. What are they going to do with it?"

Branyrd felt her heart race as she heard this. "Who told you that, sir?"

"I don't remember. He said he would not give me anymore if I told anyone where I got it."

"How long has this person been coming here to give you this stuff?" Branyrd asked as the police came out of the tent with some bags in their hands and more dynamite.

The man shrugged his shoulders and looked around in confusion.

"Sir, you need to come with us," the officer in charge said as he put handcuffs on the man.

"Please do not put him in handcuffs, Officer. He is so unsteady and cannot walk without help as it is. I can come with him for support."

"That is up to you, miss. Are you related to him?"

"No, but I am here to help in any way I can."

The man patted Branyrd's hand as she assisted him to the police cruiser and sat in back with him. She waved at Lucas to come over. "Please do what you can to find his sister and tell her what is happening here."

"Okay. I'll do that right away, Branyrd," Lucas responded, wondering how he was going to do that.

As the cruiser drove away from the scene, Branyrd heard Benedicto's whispered voice in her head and felt his hand on her shoulder. She looked around. "Where are you?"

"I'm right beside you, Branyrd. No one else can see me but you," he winked at her and smirked with a raised crooked brow.

"I see you now. What are we going to do?" she whispered in her head back to the Guardian Angel.

"HE will tell us soon. No worries, Angel."

The officers were doing their own whispering in the front seat about the find. "How did we miss that guy's tent? He had a few bags of Oxycodone and other drugs we need to identify. There was even a used needle under his pillow. I was afraid to touch it even with gloves. The whole tent area was filthy too and stunk so bad I had to hold my breath."

"I know what you mean. They should burn the whole place down, tents included, to rid the neighborhood of the stink."

"Hey, don't talk like that. These people are human beings who are in need. We have no idea what they have gone through to get to this level of degradation," the kind officer replied with annoyance.

"Yeah, right!" the unsympathetic officer replied with a guffaw.

"If you can't say anything kind, don't say anything at all!" the caring officer said with finality.

Branyrd listened to this exchange and sighed in relief that at least one of these officers had a heart. Maybe this poor man, whatever his name is, will be taken care of by at least one of the officers. She would make sure he was treated with kindness and would stay by his side until his sister could be located to take over. If Lucas couldn't find her…then she would have to become his caregiver.

***

Lucas tried to locate the woman he had seen by wracking his brain over everything she had said when they had first met. He finally remembered she was living in the next town over when she had mentioned that she had a twenty-minute drive there by the highway. She also said her name was Sanora…something. He went to see Nick who had a cell phone to try to look up the name Sanora. It wasn't a common name, maybe something would come up.

After several tries Lucas found a few Sanora's spread over the state. He called the first two without any luck until he reached the last one. This Sanora answered and almost hung up with him when he had mentioned her brother was a homeless person.

"Wait a minute, Sanora. We met one time when you visited your brother. My name is Lucas. Do you remember? Your brother is in trouble. He has been arrested and is at the local police station in Archer, New Hampshire. Can you come right away? My boss, Branyrd, is there with him for support."

"What did Brett do?"

"Brett. Is that his name? No one knew his name. He never told us," Lucas stated as he continued to explain, "Brett had some drugs in his tent along with a few sticks of dynamite."

"Drugs, I understand but dynamite? What would he be doing with dynamite? He could have blown himself and the rest of you up? What was he thinking? Oh, I know, he doesn't!" Sanora exclaimed in disgust. "What do you expect me to do now? He has made a miserable mess of his life. How can I fix it for him? I think it's too late."

"No, it is never too late, Sanora. You are his only relative and last hope to find his way back from all this. Right? You can't abandon him now," Lucas begged.

"Yes, I am his own living relative, but what do you expect me to do, Lucas? I felt helpless to do anything with him all this time. What makes you think he will accept my help now?"

"He is family, Sanora. He needs you. I think he would be more than happy to see you. Did you know he asked my boss, Branyrd, if she was his sister who had come to see him?"

Sanora took a sharp intact of breath and sighed with a choked voice, "I didn't know that. He was looking for me?"

"Yes, I think he never stopped looking for you," Lucas exaggerated in hopes of convincing her to come.

"Okay. I will be there as soon as I can. Give me the address of the police station. Thank you, Lucas, for reaching out to me. I had given up hope but now maybe there is still a chance for Brett."

Lucas gave her the address and said, "You are welcome, Sanora. Thank you. Let me know if I can help in any way."

"Okay. Thanks again."

Lucas let out a deep sigh of relief after ending the call and looked at Nick giving him a thumbs up.

"She is coming, Nick. Thank God. I didn't know what we would do if she refused. Poor Branyrd is stuck there until Sanora arrives."

"Branyrd is an Angel of a woman, she would help the most decrepit of souls. She is one good person to have on our side."

"Yeah, I agree, Nick. She is a special person in every way, kind, caring, sensitive to others' needs and generous to a fault. I wonder how we were so lucky to have her here to help us."

"I guess someone up there must like us, Lucas. Right?" Nick said with a snicker.

"Maybe," Nick said as he shook his head in disbelief.

CHAPTER THIRTY

Back at the police station Branyrd spoke on the man's behalf. She didn't really know anything about him except that he had a sister who she hoped her friend, Lucas, would locate soon.

"What is going to happen to this poor man?" Branyrd asked anxiously.

"Well, he will be fingerprinted and put in a cell until we can find out anything else from him. We do not want him. We want his supplier. Once he sobers up, he may remember who that person is. We can offer him a way out of this if he cooperates."

"Doesn't he need a lawyer?" Branyrd pushed further.

"He should get one but do you think he is in any way able to do that or even be able to afford one?" the officer asked with a furrowed brow.

"I guess not. Can I use your phone, Officer? I will see what I can do for him."

Before Branyrd was given a phone, a woman's raised voice could be heard outside the room.

"I am his sister. Let me in to see him. I am his lawyer."

Branyrd jumped up and left the room to see the woman who was upset.

The policeman let the woman go to her brother's cell and she and Branyrd almost collided. "Sorry about that," Branyrd said as she put out her hands to stop the woman from moving any further.

"Who are you?" the woman asked Branyrd.

"I am a friend of your brother's. I came here with him when he was arrested."

"Oh, I see. Thank you. How do you know my brother?" the woman looked at Branyrd with a wrinkled brow.

Branyrd explained, "I met him when I came to help the homeless community."

"You came here to help them? Why? They are all hopeless. I tried so many years to help him. He did not want it and pushed me away. I finally stopped trying to change him."

"Yes, I understand how that can happen. Families feel helpless and do not know what to do. Have you been back to the community lately?"

"No, but when I got the call I came right away. Lucas called me to tell me what my brother had done. Where did he get the drugs and dynamite? Why would he have dynamite? Drugs I can understand."

"That is what we are trying to figure out. He is completely out of it right now. He must have taken some of the drugs recently. I have not seen him like this since I have been here."

"Pardon me, let me introduce myself. I am Sanora, Brett's sister."

"Oh, his name is Brett. No one in the community knows his name. That is nice to put a name to his kind face. I am Branyrd. Sorry I did not tell you sooner. It is nice to meet you, Sanora."

"Same here, Branyrd. Brett never told anyone what his name is? That is quite strange. I wonder why?" Sanora wore a puzzled expression. "Lucas did say that to me earlier."

"I wondered the same thing, Sanora."

"I need to see my brother now. He is going to need my help in a different way."

"I heard you say that you are a lawyer. Can you legally represent your own family?"

"Well, it is not legal in a sense but I can get one of my colleagues to represent him in name only. I will do all the work."

"What can I do to help?" Branyrd asked, waiting for a response.

"I do not know yet. Thank you for being here for Brett. He was not in his right mind to handle any of this on his own. You don't have to stay any longer. I will be here for him. Where can I get in touch with you, Branyrd?"

"I will be at the homeless community. I also have a phone you can reach me by," Branyrd recited the number by heart while Sanora put it into her phone.

"I will be in touch. Thanks again, Branyrd."

Branyrd returned to the main desk to ask for a ride back to the homeless community. Soon she was back there where everyone was waiting to hear what happened to the man now known as Brett.

Lucas came forward the moment Branyrd got out of the cruiser. "We thought you would never get back here, Branyrd. How is Brett doing?"

"He will be fine now that his sister is there to support him. Oh, you know his name already?"

"Yes, his sister told me."

"His sister, Sanora, told me too. Thank you for reaching her. How did you find her, by the way? Did you know she was a lawyer?"

"You're welcome. It is the least I could do. I found her online after I remembered what city she lived in and her first name. Once I contacted her, she told me that she was a lawyer. That is good to hear she is there. Poor Brett. I wonder how he got involved with the drugs and now dynamite? I never saw him like he was today. He was always out of it a little but not stoned."

"Hmm, that's odd, isn't it, Lucas? Someone gave him those drugs recently then."

"Right. I think he mostly drank when he could get something from the others. I think he also had a prescription for sleeping pills. I do not know how he even got that," Lucas stated in a surprised voice. "Maybe his sister got him the prescription."

"Yeah, maybe she did, which I doubt though. But she seemed to be upset with him since he refused to let her help him in any way in the past. I hope he allows her to help him now. I do not want to see him go to prison."

"I agree, Branyrd. I don't think he will. She appears to be an intelligent woman who can handle this situation."

"I hope so, Lucas. How's things going in the other stores?"

"Come see for yourself, Branyrd. Everyone has been keeping busy to keep their minds from what has happened to Brett. I will tell them his name so we don't have to call him our friend anymore even though he still is."

"Okay, lead the way, Lucas. I can't wait to see it!"

When Lucas opened the door to the new construction, Branyrd gasped in surprise. "Wow, this looks incredible, guys! Thank you so much. You really have outdone yourselves."

The walls were all up and painted with shelving for supplies, beds nestled against the walls with a row of lockers for the occupants to store their belongings. This was going to be the new housing area. More bathrooms were being installed for both men and women next the showers that were already there along with a laundromat with several machines at the ready.

Branyrd walked through the doorway to another area which was going to house the café. Long tables were set up with chairs, a kitchen area was being built with a huge countertop while stove and refrigerator openings were there waiting for the deliveries.

She could not believe how large everything was now that they had opened the walls between the meeting area and the café. There would now be a place for the homeless to meet and greet one another and then sit down and eat. It would serve as a soup kitchen for them.

The Marines had set up a small library area with seating they had built into the wall overlooking the street view. There was plenty of sun coming in making it feel quite cozy. They had thought of everything.

Branyrd felt tears of joy brimming in her eyes as she looked around at all that had been done with such precision and a heavy dose of love for the community.

She called out to Nick to come over so she could talk to him. He looked up and hurried over to see her. "Is everything okay with our friend, Branyrd?"

Lucas interjected, "His name is Brett, Nick. We just found out from his sister."

"Oh, that's good. It felt a little strange to keep calling him, my friend," Nick responded with relief.

"Yes, he is doing okay now that his sister is with him. She will make sure he doesn't go to prison since she is a lawyer."

"Well, that is fortunate." Nick waited for Branyrd to say something else.

"That isn't all I wanted to say to you, Nick. I want to thank you, Lucas and the rest of the Marines and others for all the hard work that is exceptional in every way. I can't believe you did all this in such a short time. You are all quite talented. Nice to see you put those talents to good use."

"Thank you, Branyrd. We were worried about…our …Brett. Happy to hear he is being taken care of for now. Hope he gets back here to reap the rewards of our work."

"Oh, I think he will. Don't worry," Branyrd said after a quick, silent prayer.

"How soon before we can get everyone inside, Nick?"

"It won't be long. We have to supply the new beds with sheets, blankets, etc. and toiletries in the bathrooms, food on the shelves and install the appliances. Most of this will be done next week. My buddies promised to work around the clock until it is all completed. Cam has been a great help in getting everything inspected and deliveries coming in a timely fashion."

"That's sensational, Nick! Thank you and Cam too. I'm sure you will miss doing all this but soon you will have your own business. Right?"

"We hope to, Branyrd. We have received calls about some jobs locally but we need to find a place for our business first."

"Why don't you use one of the buildings here that are not being used. We have enough space right now for you to do that."

"We could use the end building which is too small for anything else. But we don't own it, you do, Branyrd. Can we buy it from you or pay rent?"

"No."

"No?"

"Of course, you can, Nick. What I was going to say was that you will not have to buy it just pay rent each month to the fund that Lucas will be handling for the community. I will give it to you with that stipulation for all you have done for this community so unselfishly without pay. I will get someone to draw up the plans so you can take it over as a renter with copies to you and Lucas who will be your landlord. We just need a lawyer."

"It looks like you may have someone who can do that, Branyrd." Lucas pointed to the woman who was heading their way.

"Hi Sanora. Is Brett doing better?"

"Yes, he is coming out of it now and sobering up. He understands why he is in jail but doesn't remember who gave him the drugs or dynamite."

"That's too bad. Will the police let him out?"

"Yes, I am going to leave him there overnight to sleep it off and pick him up tomorrow. I can bring him back home with me if he wants to leave here. By the looks of this place, he may want to stay though. It looks so different! Quite impressive! Who did all the work?"

Nick stepped forward and introduced himself. "Hi, I'm Nick and in charge of the building construction under Lucas's directions." He looked at Lucas and winked.

"My brother told me about how much you all have done to make the homeless community a better place. Thank you for all you have done. Brett is sorry to disappoint you all but promises to get his life back in order."

"We all love Brett. We look forward to his return. I have a special place just for him. Look around, Sanora, and see what we have completed," Nick said as he spread his arms around him and pointed out the specifics.

"I think I know where Brett is going to want to claim as his own place," Sanora walked over to the bed against the wall that looked out on the street with a ray of sunshine on the bed.

"Yep, that is the one I am saving for him. I hope he loves it. We gave each person a little space around their bed with storage drawers under each bed and a locker close by against the wall. We built a shelf at the headboard for them to put books and stuff with a sliding door and a key if they want to lock something up for safe keeping."

"Nice, I see that. Clever construction, Nick. I could use you to do some remodeling in my office like that."

"Well, just let me know. When we are finished here my buddies and I will be opening our own business doing remodeling and other jobs."

"That's fantastic, Nick! Let me know when you are officially open for business. I want to be one of your first customers," Sanora stated as she handed him her card.

"You can call me at the office or at my home. I put that number on the back. I wish you much success and good luck but I don't think you need luck."

"Everyone needs some good luck, Sanora, but thank you. I will be in touch," Nick said, turned and went back to work.

"Sanora, I may need your help putting together paperwork on a store at the end of the block here. I want to give Nick his start for his business. Can you prepare the paperwork to turn the store over to him for me?"

"I don't see why not, Branyrd. I would be more than happy to do that for you. Do you have the paperwork on the store?"

"Yes, let me get it for you." Branyrd returned shortly and handed it Sanora. "Let me know how much this will cost."

"Great. I will get it back to you tomorrow. Happy to help you, Branyrd, no charge after what you did for my brother. He did say to tell you he appreciated that you came with him to the police station. He remembers that you were there holding his hand."

"Thank you, that's kind of you, Sanora. But I can afford to pay you. Oh, how sweet of Brett. I felt he needed a friend and I was there to support him."

"No, I won't take anything from you. See you tomorrow, Branyrd." Sanora waved and drove away.

Branyrd sighed and whispered Benedicto's name. He appeared beside her and touched her arm. "Are you okay, little Angel?"

"Yes, it was only a sigh of satisfaction, Benedicto. I feel we are almost at the end of my mission. Right?"

"Well, soon anyway, Branyrd. There are still a few things you must take care of before we leave."

"What? Did I forget something important?"

Before Benedicto could answer her, a crash was heard coming from the alley way.

Branyrd and Benedicto rushed over there, being the only ones who had heard the crash. There was so much hammering and banging going on inside the stores no one took notice of the sound of a crash.

CHAPTER THIRTY-ONE

Ezra was inside his tent bedroom and poked his head out to see what made the noise. "Who are you?" he asked the man who was knocking over garbage cans.

"Where did you come from, little boy?" the man asked, looking around him in confusion.

Before Ezra could answer Branyrd and Benedicto were beside him protecting him from harm.

"Who are you, sir?" Branyrd asked as she kept Ezra behind her.

"I was looking for something. I am no one."

"What did you lose, sir?" Benedicto stepped forward.

"I…I…don't remember."

"You don't remember what you lost and you are looking for it. How can you find it if you do not know what that is?" Benedicto queried further and walked closer to the man.

"I…don't…" After one look at Benedicto the man ran away before finishing his sentence.

"Who was that man, Aunt Branyrd?" Ezra asked. "I was going to tell him about my tent but he didn't stay long enough. "What was he looking for?"

"I don't know, Ezra, but Benedicto will go see what is inside the garbage can."

Benedicto picked up the can and looked inside. At the bottom of the can was a stick of dynamite and a bottle of liquid. There were some in the other cans the man had knocked over. He also saw a line of white powder leading away from the cans. Benedicto blew it up into the air so it wouldn't connect to the cans.

"Is it what I think it is, Benedicto?"

"Yes, I will dispose of what is in the cans. Take Ezra away from here and don't let anyone down the alley until I say it is safe."

"Yes, right away, Benedicto. Come with me Ezra. I think your daddy is looking for you."

"Daddy told me to go to my bed and read my book and that he would be coming back soon."

"Do you like the book, Ezra?" Branyrd asked to get Ezra's mind off of the man.

"Yes, I love the stories about the bear and the boy. They are friends, you know. But will my book disappear with our bedroom?" Ezra asked, suddenly remembering he left it inside the box bedroom.

"No. I won't let that happen, Ezra."

"Okay. I didn't want to lose my book," Ezra sighed in relief.

"Are the bear and boy friends in the book?" Branyrd smiled, pleased to see Ezra so happy with his book.

"Yes, they are the very best of friends. I will have friends too because Daddy said I am going to go to school soon. He found a place for us to live and the school is close to our apartment."

"Really? That's terrific!"

Branyrd walked Ezra back to the stores where his father was talking to Nick. Lucas looked up in surprise to see Branyrd with Ezra in tow.

"What's going on? Why are you out of bed, Ezra?"

"He's fine. We need to talk, Lucas. Ezra, go inside to see if you can help the Marines. Okay?" Branyrd instructed as she led Lucas away from his son.

"What happened, Branyrd? I can see something did by the look on your face."

"It's all okay now. Benedicto is taking care of everything in the alley. There was a loud sound a little while ago. I guess no one heard it but us. There was a man who was putting dynamite and liquid in several of the garbage cans in the process of lighting fuses to set them off."

"Oh my God! Ezra was inside the tent reading. I told him to go there to take a nap."

"He is fine. Don't worry. We took care of it. Benedicto will find the man and bring him to the police."

"Who was he? Why was he doing this?"

"I don't know who he is but I think I know who is behind this."

"Tell me, Branyrd. Who would want to hurt any of us. My son could have been killed!"

"But he is fine. I wouldn't let anything happen to any of you. I promise, Lucas."

"I know. I believe you. But what if you weren't here to hear that sound and go to the rescue?"

"But we were here. It's all over now. Relax. Okay? We will check out the alley every night from now on."

"Okay. I don't know how to thank you, Branyrd. Ezra is my world. I wouldn't know…"

"I understand, Lucas. Listen, Ezra told me you found a place to stay so he can go to school."

"Yes. He is so excited about going to school. I can't live here with him. It's not right. It's okay for others but not for a young child like him."

"I agree, Lucas. Good for you that you are finding your way to a new life. I am proud of all you have accomplished. What about Amy? Are you still working in her store?"

"Yes, part-time now since I have been helping Nick with the stores. We need to get finished so everyone can have a place to stay out of the cold."

"You will finish it, I'm sure. Then what about Amy?"

"We are dating if that's what you mean, Branyrd."

"Well, I was curious. She is a nice young woman and Ezra seems to like her a lot."

"Yes, we both do. But I still have to find my wife and settle things with her. I want a divorce. Ezra understands that too."

"I think he does. He said recently that he wants a divorce from his mother. He is too precious."

"He is quite a character, isn't he?" Lucas chuckled.

"Out of the mouths of babes, they say," Branyrd said with a giggle.

"Yes. He is a special little boy. We are planning to give him a surprise birthday party in the finished café. That's why we are working overtime to get it done. He doesn't expect anything."

"No, I don't think he does. Benedicto and I were planning a little surprise for him too. Let me know when you are ready and we will bring what we have for him to the party. Let us know if there is anything else you need. In fact, let us pick up a cake and other decorations. Benedicto is good at coming up with all kinds of things in a wink of an eye."

"That's nice of both of you. Thank you, Branyrd. I hadn't thought about the cake. Ezra will be pleased with whatever you give him. He likes you both. He keeps telling me you are both probably Angels."

"Really? How sweet of him." Branyrd raised her eyebrows at these words.

CHAPTER THIRTY-TWO

Mayor Cramston was upset with Alice. "Where were you, Alice? I have been calling you on the phone."

"I was in the lady's room. I am human, Mayor, and have needs that can't wait forever. What is it that is so important?"

"I need some paperwork on the homeless community. Who owns those buildings they are working on now?"

"I think Branyrd does," Alice replied, hesitantly.

"When did she purchase them? Get me the owners of those buildings on the phone now. Something is fishy here."

Alice shuffled some papers around on her desk after ending the call to her boss. She picked up the phone and quickly called Branyrd.

"Hi Alice. What's up? You sound funny."

"It's the mayor, Branyrd. He is asking about who owns the property you are working on. I think he is going to cause you some trouble."

"No problem, Alice, I own all the property along with Lucas. It is all legal and binding."

"Oh, thank goodness. I was worried that he would throw a wrench into things. He is nothing but trouble. But I think his time is waning."

"What do you mean, Alice?" Branyrd asked with curiosity as she waited for an answer.

"He has taken things too far and made enemies of some powerful people. Time will tell. He will not be here much longer."

"What has he done?"

"Well, he purchased some dynamite recently. I saw the order on his desk before he picked it up and pushed it into his drawer. He also hired some thugs to do his bidding. I do not know what they did but I'm sure it isn't anything legal. Remember the man that I told you came to my office? I think he is part of the syndicate, drugs and stuff."

"Really? Hmm. I see. Thank you for letting me know, Alice. I think it is time for you to get a new job."

"I will soon. I want to stay around long enough to see him go to jail. That would make it all worthwhile," Alice snickered.

"Stay safe, Alice. Thanks again for the update."

"My pleasure, Branyrd. You all stay safe. I will do what I can on my end."

Benedicto heard the conversation and nodded to Branyrd. Well, it looks like we know who was behind the dynamite and drugs."

"Yes, we do. I will have to contact Sanora and let her know this. Her brother will be free and clear now. We need to let the police handle the mayor and his cronies once and for all."

***

Back at the mayor's office three men came in to see Mayor Cramston. Alice greeted them and asked, "Do you have an appointment?"

"No, sorry we don't. But it is urgent we speak with him."

Alice admired the three men who were dressed in casual clothes that were neat and pressed. They were large men with well developed muscles that were evident in their shirts that clung to each muscle making Alice hold her breath a little too long. What was pleasant besides their muscles was their good manners when speaking to her. She smiled and said, "What do you need to see the mayor about, gentlemen?"

One especially handsome young man stepped forward and announced, "We have something to share with the mayor about the homeless community and the problems they are having there."

"Oh, are they having problems there?"

"Yes, Ma'am, they are."

"Let me see if the mayor can see you. Please take a seat and I will get right back to you." Alice left the room and knocked on the mayor's door before entering.

A few minutes later the mayor came out with a wide smile and an outstretched hand. "What can I do for you good gentlemen?"

"My name is Kayden and I represent the other businesses in the community neighboring the homeless area. We want to help the city get back to full health again by helping Branyrd and her associates finish their renovations for the homeless. But we noticed there have been problems there with interference by outside sources. Do you know anything about this matter, Mr. Mayor?"

"Well…please come to my office so we can discuss this in private. Right this way."

The three men tipped their baseball caps to Alice and followed the mayor.

Alice gave them a reassuring smile, watching them until the mayor soundly closed the door after giving Alice a frown of exasperation.

She tiptoed closer to the door and put her ear against it hoping to find out what this was all about. She wanted to have a new scoop for Branyrd.

Raised voices were suddenly heard as Alice had to back away from the door with the force and power of them. The loudest one was the mayor when he began to yell at the men.

"Who do you think you are threatening me like that? I am the mayor of this city. I control everything that goes on here. You, do not! Just because you own businesses in my city doesn't give you the right to tell me what to do!"

"Mr. Mayor, we are not trying to tell you what to do, we only want to ensure the people in the homeless community are safe from harm. We heard someone came and planted dynamite in the garbage cans and inside one of the tents that could have injured or even killed many people in the area." Cam had reported this to his fellow business owners.

"What is your name and what business do you own?" Mayor Cramston directed his attention to the man who was doing all the talking.

"My name is Kayden and I own the Kayden's Department Store."

"Hmm, I see. I have never shopped there and won't in the future. I think you had better keep your opinions to yourself, Kayden, and let me run my city."

"I'm sorry to hear that I won't be seeing you in my store. My friends in the State House will be sorry also to hear about how you are running this city into the ground. I have many friends in high places, sir, whom you will have to explain why you are ignoring the problems right in front of you."

"What? Get out of my office, now!!"

The three men got up and left the office without another word but did stop by Alice's desk to thank her, "We appreciate you giving us time with the mayor." Looking at her name plate on her desk Kayden added, "Thank you, Alice. If you ever need a job, call me. I think you could do better than working for this man." Kayden handed her his card and walked away. The other two men tipped their caps and smiled at her making her day.

Alice looked at the card and smiled. *What a nice name he has – Kayden, to go along with the beautiful smile.*

Mayor Cramston came barreling out of his office, sweating profusely, and stopped at Alice's desk. Get me the governor on the phone right away."

"Yes, Mayor, right away." Alice smirked to herself.

Right after she connected her boss with the governor, she called Branyrd.

"Hi Alice. You sound upset. Is everything all right?" Branyrd asked, knowing that it was not. She hadn't told Alice about what was happening at the community lately.

"Well, there were three young men here, very attractive and well-built young men by the way, who came to see the mayor. There was yelling and arguments back and forth. These men came to ask the mayor why he wasn't keeping his city safe for the homeless community. You didn't tell me there was trouble there again, Branyrd, even after I told you about the men who the mayor hired to cause trouble."

"I know, Alice. I didn't want to upset you. Everything is all right here now. The police have taken care of it."

"Well, as long as no one was hurt. I am quitting once again. I cannot take this man and his evil ways. One of the men, Kayden, is his name, gave me his card in case I wanted a different job. I may take him up on it. If only I was thirty years younger, he was quite a hunk!"

Branyrd giggled at Alice's remark and said, "Well, I hope you find a better job than the one you have and with a nicer boss. Thank you for keeping me in the loop, Alice. I'm sorry I didn't do the same for you. Please keep in touch and let me know how you are doing in your new job."

"Oh, I definitely will, Branyrd. Maybe I'll stop by sometime to see how things are progressing there. I heard you have done much more since I was last there."

"Yes, we have. Lucas and Nick have done a tremendous job with all the renovations and additions. It is quite beautiful! They love to show it off to anyone who is interested."

"Also, I have to tell you that all the people in this building have been giving more for your fund. I will drop it off to the bank for you and deposit it into the account. Okay?"

"Sure, that would be wonderful. Thank you. We are in the process of finishing Nick's office at the end of the block."

"Nick's office?"

"Oh, right, you did not know about Nick going into the woodworking and renovation business. He and his fellow Marines who have done all this work are going into business together and using the last building on the block. I plan to have Nick pay rent to Lucas for the use of the building he will be using for his business."

"Wow, that's great! Nick and his buddies are talented men. I love what they did in the buildings! Tell Nick I wish him much success in whatever he endeavors to do."

"Thank you, Alice. I will, but you could tell him yourself when you visit us soon."

"Okay, I promise I will come soon. Take care, Branyrd."

"You too, Alice."

Alice picked up the card and made another call – this one would change her life.

CHAPTER THIRTY-THREE

Governor Crosley did not like Mayor Cramston and always thought of him as a pompous asshole. When his secretary told him the mayor was on the line, he took a deep breath and answered.

"Mr. Mayor, how are you?"

"Governor Crosley, I don't have time for pleasantries. I have something to discuss with you."

"You never do, Mayor."

"What did you say?"

"What do you have to discuss with me?"

"Three men came into my office a few minutes ago and threatened me."

"What do you mean threatened you? In what way?"

"They don't like the way I run the city. They think they can do better."

He whispered, "I bet they could."

"What did you say, Crosley?"

"Oh, why did they say that, Cramston?"

"I don't know. I guess it's because of the homeless community troubles. I've tried to help them but they are useless and helpless."

"Hmm, I see. I've heard about how the homeless will soon not be homeless. That's a good thing, isn't it, Mayor?"

"Maybe or maybe not. They will only end up on the street again. Some of them are beyond help anyway and on their way out."

"Then it's your job to make sure they are comfortable until that time. You don't want to rush them into graves, do you? It appears to me you have a miracle in the works by the looks of the renovations that have taken place."

"How do you know about that?"

"I sent some of my people over there this morning to look it over. They texted me some photos of what has been done. It's quite impressive. I plan to go there today to see it for myself. This is a good thing for our state and for your city. You should be proud and encourage those people who are doing all that work without pay. I donated to their cause myself. You should do the same, Mayor."

"But...but..."

"Is there anything else you must add, Mayor? If not, I have a trip to make. Good day."

***

Back at the homeless community Branyrd met with four people that said they represented Governor Crosley's office. "Hello, we are here at the request of the governor. He wanted to see how you were doing with the homeless community renovations. He told us to tell you he is quite proud of what you have accomplished without any pay, credit or help from the mayor. He wants to see this for himself later today."

"Nice to meet you all. Thank you for coming. I will personally thank the governor for his support and compliments when I see him. Please come this way and I will introduce you to the planning and construction managers."

Lucas and Nick met the governor's contingent and explained what they had completed so far. There were oohs and aahs all around as they took in the carpentry and remodeling that was on display in all the rooms throughout the buildings that were now connected.

Branyrd stepped aside to let Lucas and Nick take over the tour. She knew the governor's people were in good hands.

She sighed and looked up for guidance. "What do I do now, LORD? Is it almost time for me to leave? Have I done all that YOU expected of me? Are YOU happy with my work here?"

"Angel, you have gone above and beyond my expectations. You have done a commendable job, little Angel. I am pleased with you in every way."

"Thank you, LORD. I am happy but sad at the same time knowing I must leave these people. I don't think they need me anymore. They are doing everything on their own now."

"That is all because of you, Angel. You were the instrument that directed the players who thus made the music so beautiful."

"Wow, that was lovely to hear. Thank you. I am awestruck. I don't feel I did anything out of the ordinary. I didn't even use my powers too often. The only thing that I can't do yet is disappear like Benedicto."

"Don't be too sure about that, Angel. You can do anything you put your mind to, never forget that. See you soon."

"Yes, LORD. I will keep that in mind and keep working on the disappearance stuff. Oh, but how soon, LORD?"

Branyrd looked up and around but HE was gone. She whispered her Guardian Angel's name, "Benedicto, where are you?"

"I am here, Angel. What is it you need? Did HE not say it all?"

"Yes, HE was inspiring to say the least as always, but I need to know when I must return to Heaven. HE did not tell me. HE said, 'See you soon.' What does that mean?"

"It means it will be sooner than you think, little Angel."

"But I don't think I am ready to leave these people who have become like my family." She looked around and Benedicto was gone also. What was she going to do?

Before she could get out of her musings, she heard a voice speaking to her, "Excuse me. Are you the lady in charge here?"

She opened her eyes and saw a large, stately-looking and distinguished middle-aged man with hair graying in a pleasant way above his ears, wearing a smile and a good-looking three-piece suit standing in front of her. There were a couple of serious-looking men beside him.

"I'm sorry, I must have been daydreaming. I didn't see you. I am Branyrd. Yes, I used to be in charge but now there are others who are taking over where I left off. What can I do for you, sir?"

"I am Governor Crosley. Nice to meet you, Branyrd. I have heard so much about you in the newspapers and from my people who saw you this morning. They sent me texts about the place. They may still be here. They haven't returned to the office yet."

"I think they are still in the buildings looking over all the work that has been done. Let me take you there so you can see what these talented men have built."

"I would love to see everything that is being done to change this community into a new place for all these people to live in safety, comfort and with care. You are to be commended for undertaking something no one else has tried to do and succeeding too. I would like to honor you with a plaque for all your efforts and that of the group who supported you."

"Oh, not me, please give it to these two men and all their helpers. They are the ones who did all this. I was here to lead the way, that is all."

"I disagree, Branyrd. You are the leader of the band, so to speak, that got the group together so that they could play the music or in this case do the work to complete this unbelievable project and see it through to fruition."

Branyrd looked up and smiled, the words the LORD had said were reverberating inside the governor's head too.

"Did I say something to amuse you?"

"Oh, not at all, Governor. Your words were lovely. Please come this way and see for yourself how talented this group is and how deserving they are of a plaque and recognition."

Governor Crosley followed Branyrd into the first building and moved throughout the buildings that were connected through doorways and archways to make it easier for everyone to go from one place or another.

After introductions were finished between the governor and Lucas and Nick, the governor replied, "Well, I see what you mean, Branyrd. These men are truly talented in many ways. I could use them on construction projects for the state. They would do a much better job than the people I have now employed."

"Thank you, Governor Crosley," both Lucas and Nick exclaimed together in surprise at his words of praise.

Nick spoke up first, "Governor, I am most humbled by your kind words but I am going into business with all these men who have put their hearts and souls on the line to complete this project. We already have numerous jobs lined up to complete after we are through here. But we will do whatever you need after that. I can contact you to let you know when we will be available for any projects you may have."

The rest of the Marines nodded in agreement with smiles of confidence that they would be working for a long time without worrying about money ever again.

Governor Crosley handed Nick his card and called out to his people who were sitting in the café having a cup of coffee and a doughnut without a care in the world. "Time to go back to work. I don't want to interrupt your coffee break but it is getting late," he guffawed with a big smile.

His contingent got up and tossed their cups and napkins into the nearest bin and followed the governor out the door with a thank you and a shake of hands as they passed by Nick, Lucas and Branyrd.

"I'll be in touch, Branyrd. Take care and congratulations for a job well done."

"Thank you, Governor Crosley, for stopping by. It was a pleasure to meet you."

Nick and Lucas came aside of Branyrd and Nick remarked, "What a nice man the governor is. I had never met him, only the mayor. Thank goodness he is nothing like Mayor Cramston."

"Ha, that's a good thing for sure, Nick. I think the governor knows how cantankerous and condescending the mayor is and how uncooperative and unsupportive he has been to us," Lucas stated with a guffaw.

"Yes, I think Kayden had something to do with the governor coming here according to Alice," Branyrd stated.

"Really, the Kayden we know from the local businessmen who came here to support us?" Lucas queried.

"Yes, the very same one. He and a couple of others paid a visit to the mayor recently. Whatever they said stirred up the pot and the governor came to see what it was all about," Branyrd said. "Just don't spread word that Alice told us any of this."

"I won't. I understand. But it's good for us that we have Governor Crosley on our side," Lucas exclaimed in relief. "The mayor is nothing but trouble. He doesn't want us to succeed. I don't understand why not though."

"I think I do, Lucas. He tried in the past to do something about this homeless community and failed. He did not want anyone else to succeed because it would make him look bad and remind people of his failure."

"I see, Branyrd. You know all this because of Alice. She is the leader of the gossip mill in the city."

"I guess you could say that, Lucas. Remember to keep that quiet about her, okay? I don't think she will be staying with the mayor much longer though so we will lose our grapevine of gossip."

"Sure thing, Branyrd. Mums the word. Where is Alice going?"

"I don't know yet but I'm sure she will let me know soon."

"This will be the second time she has quit her job with the mayor," Nick said with a laugh.

"Right. But I think Alice is a bright woman who has her own mind and will succeed wherever she goes. She is getting up in age and will probably be retiring before too many years anyway," Branyrd stated.

"Good for her to finish in a position where she is happier before that time. I wish her all the best," Lucas said with a nod of agreement from Nick.

"I agree with you both. She is a lovely lady. I am happy to have met her," Branyrd replied with a sigh and a smile.

"Wait a minute, Branyrd. You sound like you are going somewhere too."

"I told you, Lucas, I am only here until everything is completed. I have other missions to begin."

"There you go with the missions again, Branyrd. What does all that mean? You can't leave us. You are the heart and soul of this operation," Lucas said with fondness.

"Right! What are we going to do without your counsel and support?" Nick inquired with a frown.

"Gentlemen, you are quite capable of continuing the music without me."

"What music?" Nick and Lucas exchanged questioning glances.

"Ha, you know what I mean. You are quite capable of handling any situation with panache and receive plenty of accolades without my help."

"I still don't know what I would have done without your help, Branyrd. I would still be sulking and dragging myself and Ezra around without getting anywhere. You are instrumental in helping me get my act together. I even have a house now and Ezra will be going to school in September of this year."

"Yes, I am thrilled to hear that. Oh, by the way I have another book for Ezra to help him learn his alphabet which you will be teaching him as you read to him each night, Lucas. Right?"

"Yes, of course. We already started doing that. I have him writing his name now. Soon he will be able to read some of the book you gave him without my prodding him along."

"Good to hear, Lucas. I am so pleased. That's perfect. Here is the book that I promised to give Ezra." Branyrd quickly pulled it out of the air and waved her hands over Lucas and Nick before they could say anything to erase their memory of her act of magic.

Lucas exclaimed in surprise as Branyrd handed it to him, "Oh, this is the second book in the **Bedtime Stories for Children Series, Make Believe is Fun.** Ezra will love it! This is so kind of you, Branyrd. Thank you. Thank you for everything."

"You are welcome, Lucas. I'm happy to be of help to you and Ezra and proud of how far you have come. There isn't anything you cannot accomplish on your own."

"Well, I don't know if I have as much confidence in myself as you do, Branyrd, but I thank you for your kind words. I feel like I have a new lease on life thanks to you."

"So do I, Branyrd. You have been at the forefront of my beginning a new business and completing all this work for such an outstanding cause. I want to do more of this to help the community. It looks like the governor will have work for us to do once we complete all the orders we have piling up now."

"I am proud of you too, Nick, and your fellow Marines for what you have done for the homeless who are no longer homeless. They are all living inside the building that is now theirs fully furnished. All you need are some finishing touches and food to be delivered."

Doc came alongside Branyrd and said, "Yes, we are getting there. I almost forgot, Branyrd. I enlisted two of my fellow Marines who were also EMTs and now are doctors. They will be putting in some time on their own to help us out with the clinic. They will round up more doctors and nurses who can donate an hour, hours, days or weekends to care for the needy ones here. I even have a woman who offered to be secretary here for us in her off hours at the hospital where she is a medical secretary."

"That's fabulous news, Doc. Thank you so much for what you have done here. My heart is full but at the same time it is sad to see it all end. I hate to leave you all. You have become my family in more ways than one."

Lucas came forward and embraced Branyrd and said, "You are my family, Branyrd, and always will be."

Nick and Doc hugged the Angel too and said, "Mine too, Branyrd. We love you."

"Thank you all. I love you like my brothers and will never forget you. I want you to know that I will be watching over you and wishing you good health, happiness and prosperity in your futures."

"Now that really does sound ominous, Branyrd," Lucas said.

"Where are you going, Aunt Branyrd?" Ezra came over to see Branyrd afraid he was missing out on something.

Branyrd caught her breath each time she heard Ezra call her aunt. "I promise I won't leave yet, Ezra. But first I have a present for you. Isn't it your birthday in a few days?"

"Yes, you remembered? What do you have for me?" Ezra asked, eagerly with curiosity.

"Here is the book I promised you." Lucas gave the book back to Branyrd and she handed it to Ezra and watched his eyes grow wider in delight.

"This is like the other book I have but in a different color and it has different animals on the cover. I love it, Aunt Branyrd. Thank you so much!"

"Your father told me that you are learning to write your name and spell it too."

"Yes, would you like me to show you. I need to get a paper and a pencil."

"Let's go inside and find them, Ezra." Branyrd smiled as she led the little boy inside the building.

Nick asked Lucas, "What was all that about leaving?"

"I don't know. She has other people to help I guess and we are almost finished here. She has been a godsend to us."

"That is for certain, Lucas. I don't know what we will do without her. Maybe we can persuade her to stay."

"Maybe but she does have a mind of her own, Nick. I think we have to be thankful that whoever sent her here to help us needs her to help others too."

"I guess that is possible, Lucas. Well, we must enjoy her presence while we can and be thankful to whoever sent her here."

"I agree with you, Lucas," Doc announced with a smile.

"If we are all in agreement, let's get back to work on your office now, Nick," Lucas stated in a more upbeat tone to dispel their feelings of sorrow at losing Branyrd.

"That sounds good to me, my friend. I can't wait to use it." Nick said as they pulled Doc along with them to help.

CHAPTER THIRTY-FOUR

A few days later the renovations on the project were completed including Nick's office with the help of everyone working around the clock. All the appliances were installed, food was plentiful in the cupboards and pictures of all those who had a part in the construction as it was being completed were hung on all the walls for everyone to see.

Another wall contained photos of all the homeless who were dressed for the occasion in their best duds with wide smiles along with Branyrd who appeared to have a halo over her head. Each person who looked at the photo wondered about that and where the light came from and why.

The food hall was decorated for Ezra's surprise birthday party while Lucas went shopping with Ezra for his present. He had to keep the boy away until all the preparations could be finished. They all wanted this to be a surprise for a special little boy who would turn five years old.

Branyrd and Benedicto had gone shopping by flying over to Kayden's Super Market for the cake and balloons and party favors. They also wanted to see Kayden and expressed their gratitude for his help.

When Kayden got word that the wonder of a woman, Branyrd, was in his store, he came rushing out of the office to greet her and the large man who accompanied her.

"Branyrd, it is a true pleasure to see you again. Thank you for everything you did to bring our community back to life. I can't believe how well business has bounced back, thanks to you. Look at all the people who are here! It's an amazing thing to see."

"You are welcome but I didn't do anything. It was all the people around me, including you, who helped to make a difference in this community. We wanted to thank you for what you did, going to see the governor."

"Governor? I didn't go see the governor. I did visit the mayor though," Kayden laughed remembering how he had gotten the mayor's ire up.

"You didn't see the governor?" Branyrd asked in surprise.

"No, but I did upset the mayor enough to make him call the governor. I bet that is what happened to get the governor involved."

"I see. Well, you must be thanked just the same for putting things in motion. Now the governor is planning to have a ceremony to officially open our community to the homeless. He will even present a plaque to the people who did all the work. He said he will tote this construction/renovation project as a template for other communities to follow to improve their areas that need help."

"That's tremendous, Branyrd, all due to your diligence, hard work, and inspiration."

Kayden looked at the large man who was standing next to Branyrd who was several inches taller than his six feet three. "I'm sorry I don't think we have met, sir."

Benedicto extended his hand to Kayden and swallowed it up in his huge palm but shook it firmly without undue pressure, much to the surprise of Kayden. "I'm Benedicto, a friend of Branyrd. I guess you could call me her bodyguard. I watch over her."

"It's a pleasure to meet you, Benedicto. Well, you certainly are a commanding presence. I don't think anyone is ever going to harm Branyrd with you around."

"You bet. Nice meeting you too, Kayden. You are a big man yourself."

"Well, this is one time that I feel small standing next to you," Kayden laughed.

Benedicto tittered too and asked where the cakes were in the store. "We have a party planned for Lucas's son, Ezra, and must get back there quickly. We need a cake with his name on it, some balloons and confetti and whatever else would make a birthday special."

"Right this way," Kayden said as he extended his arm forward.

They followed him and found everything they needed to surprise Ezra. Kayden even added some other items that the boy would love, a baseball cap, and bat and ball. Branyrd picked up a train set and some race cars that would fit on the tracks as gifts from her and Benedicto.

When they got to the register, Kayden waved them through and said, "It's on me. Please accept my thanks for everything you have done for our community. Tell Ezra happy birthday for me."

"Thank you, Kayden. We will. He will love what you gave him," Branyrd said with a smile.

Branyrd looked at Benedicto who was slipping something into the register as he waved his hands over the clerk so she wouldn't see what he was doing.

"What did you do, Benedicto?" Branyrd asked, curiously.

"Oh, nothing much, little Angel. I slipped in some money to cover everything we just purchased with a little extra for his kindness. He is not flush yet you know. He was nearly bankrupt and almost closed his store."

"How do you know that, Benedicto?" Branyrd queried with a frown.

"I have ways, Branyrd. I have ways. I didn't want him to have to scrape to cover our costs even though they were not too extravagant."

"That's kind of you, Benedicto. I felt uncomfortable too not paying for our purchases. Good thinking on your part."

"Time is wasting, Branyrd, let me fly us back."

"Okay by me but don't take off...oof! You didn't wait for me to say, don't take off so fast, Benedicto!"

"That was fast? Are you kidding me. That was my slow speed takeoff."

"Oh boy, I hope you never use the fast one with me. I may have a heart attack even though I don't have a heart, so to speak."

"If you did have one it would be the biggest one yet, little Angel."

"Aww, thanks, Benedicto. You too!"

"Here we are. I landed in the alleyway so they wouldn't see us."

"Good thinking! Let's get inside quickly before Lucas comes back with Ezra."

A half hour later after just enough time to get everything in order Lucas appeared with Ezra. Everyone yelled out, Happy Birthday, Ezra! The moment the little boy saw the colorful balloons, cake and presents laid out on the long table with everyone standing around, he screamed out in joy and jumped up and down hugging everyone in sight. His smile was so wide that everyone thought his face would split.

Ezra's eyes sparkled with delight and gave his father an extra hug saying, "Did you do this, Daddy?"

"No, everyone else did this. Benedicto and Branyrd did all the shopping for supplies, the cake, balloons, decorations and confetti."

"We have confetti too? Thank you so much, Aunt Branyrd and Uncle Benedicto," he exclaimed as he hugged them again and again as he couldn't stop giggling.

Benedicto's face showed his surprise and delight at being called uncle. He grinned and glanced at Branyrd who nodded in agreement.

"Do you want to have some cake or open your presents first, Ezra?" his father asked him.

"I would love some cake. I haven't had any cake in my whole life!"

"Oh, Ezra, you are too funny!" Lucas snickered. "Okay, let's have some cake. But first we have to light your five candles so you can make a wish and blow them out."

"Okay, let's do that, Daddy. I can't wait to taste this yummy cake!"

Benedicto stepped forward with a lighter and picked up Ezra to seat him in front of the cake so he could light the candles.

Everyone began to sing, 'Happy Birthday to You,' and waited for Ezra to make his wish and blow out the candles.

Before he could blow them out Benedicto whispered into the boy's ear and Ezra looked up and nodded to him. Ezra raised his hands over the cake and clapped them quickly over the flames, being careful not to touch them as the flames went out.

Everyone clapped in surprise as Ezra smiled and smiled and smiled.

"Can I open my presents now, Daddy?"

"Go for it, Ezra!"

"Yippee!" Ezra yelled as he grabbed the first present and ripped the paper into shreds throwing it on the floor. His father rolled his eyes over this but began to pick up all the pieces and toss them into a nearby bucket.

When all the presents were opened and everyone was thanked with another hug, Ezra announced, "I can't believe you remembered my birthday! I was really surprised! I love the chocolate cake, Aunt Branyrd and Uncle Benedicto. Thank you."

"You are welcome, little man," Benedicto ruffled the boy's curls.

"It was our pleasure to give you a special birthday, Ezra. I'm so happy you like what we gave you. The owner of Kayden's Department Store gave you the baseball cap, bat and ball." Branyrd said.

"Really? I don't even know him. I will have to thank him sometime. I love the train set and racing cars. Can you help me put it together, Aunt Branyrd?"

"Sure, but Uncle Benedicto is probably better at that than I am," Branyrd announced with a smirk at Benedicto.

Benedicto nodded and picked up the huge box with Ezra close behind and put it down on an area of the floor away from everyone.

Lucas came over to Branyrd and said, "I can't thank you both enough for all you did to make this possible for Ezra. I have never seen him so happy. He will remember this day and both of you for a long time, I hope."

"It was our pleasure to do this. Ezra is such a special little boy. We love him and think of him as a nephew."

"That is sweet of both of you. It was also very generous of Kayden to give him the baseball, bat and cap too. I will have to stop by his store so Ezra can thank him in person."

"Yes, Kayden is a kind and thoughtful person. He is thrilled his business is picking up and he is doing so well since you completed this project. You have helped to improve the neighborhood in a big way."

"Not me, Branyrd, you did all this. If it wasn't for your innovation, support and ingenuity to raise money for all this we wouldn't be here right now."

"I couldn't have done any of it without your help and without HIS support."

"Who do you mean?"

"The LORD of course, Lucas. We cannot do anything without HIS help."

"Oh, I see. Are you telling me I should start believing more, going to church and praying?"

"I think that would please HIM."

"Okay, I will do that soon, Branyrd. I must give HIM thanks too for sending you here to us. HE did, didn't HE?"

"Yes, HE did send me. I must be leaving soon too. HE has other missions for me to complete."

"I...I will miss you, Branyrd. I have begun to think of you as my little sister. Will I see you again sometime?"

"No…I cannot come back. I'm sorry, Lucas. I feel close to you too as my big brother. But I promise to watch over you and Ezra for as long as HE lets me."

"I don't understand any of this about watching over us and why you won't come back but I guess I have to accept what you say is true."

"Thank you, Lucas, for understanding. I can't say any more about it."

Before Lucas could say anything else he heard a familiar voice behind him.

CHAPTER THIRTY-FIVE

Lucas turned in shock when he saw his wife, Kiley, standing at the doorway.

"Kiley? What…where…how?"

Lucas was at a loss for words. He stared and slowly moved closer to her.

She put her arms out to him but he didn't go into them. He stood close by and shook his head. "Where have you been all this time? Why didn't you come back? Why did you leave Ezra with Ruby? How could you? How do you think I felt coming home to find you gone and my son with a stranger?"

"I'm…I'm…sorry, Lucas. I wasn't well back then. It has taken me all this time to heal and feel myself again. I couldn't take care of myself so how could I take care of our son?"

"I don't understand why you didn't at least try to contact me. What do you think you did to our son? He has been upset that you left him and never came back."

"Well, I came back now."

"A little too late. How did you know where to find me?"

"I saw your photo in the newspaper about this place and how you almost single-handedly put it all together."

"I didn't do all this on my own. I had many others who helped do construction and one woman who deserves all the credit." Turning around he called out to Branyrd, "Please come over here. I would like to introduce you to my... wife."

Branyrd came over with a quizzical expression on her angelic face. "Your wife?"

"Yes, this is Kylie. Kylie, this is Branyrd. She is the brains behind all this. We would not have done any of this without her support and guidance."

"Hi Branyrd. Nice to meet you," Kylie said with an outstretched hand.

"Hi Kylie. It's a pleasure to meet you too. Does Ezra know you are here?" Branyrd looked over to where Benedicto and Ezra were setting up the train set deep in conversation. She noticed Kylie's eyes were not quite focused and looked dull.

"Not yet. Where is Ezra?" Kylie asked, looking around the room. Once she spotted him, she called out, "Ezra?"

Ezra raised his head when he recognized his mother's voice and raced over to see her with arms outstretched. "Mommy, where have you been? I've missed you! You missed my birthday party. Come see my presents and play with me. Uncle Benedicto helped me set up my train set. Look at it! It's beautiful, isn't it?"

"Oh Ezra, my baby boy. How big you have grown. Let me hold you a little longer. It has been so long since I have held you." Tears filled Kylie's eyes as she kept Ezra in a tight grip as he tried to wiggle his way out to go back to his train.

"I must help Uncle Benedicto. Come with me, Mommy." Ezra grabbed his mother's hand before she could refuse and pulled her along. Once they were settled with the train set, Benedicto excused himself, left the building and disappeared.

Branyrd watched her Guardian Angel in action doing this and shook her head. Where is he going?

"What's wrong, Branyrd? You look upset," Lucas inquired.

"Oh nothing, Lucas. I was only wondering how Kylie found you and where she has been all this time?"

"She saw my photo in the newspaper with an article about this place. She also said she has been getting better, probably in rehab or some place like that. It took her all this time to find us. I don't know whether to believe her or not. She could have at least called me or inquired about our son when we were still in our apartment. No word for two years," Lucas sighed heavily and shook his head back and forth as his eyes brimmed.

Branyrd touched him on his back and said in almost a whisper, "Everything is going to be all right, Lucas. Take a deep breath and try to relax."

"I can't relax. I am upset with her and still want a divorce. She is not fit to be a mother. No mother would do what she did without a word."

"I understand that you feel this way but you must give her a chance to explain and spend some time with your son. She looks penitent and happy to be with him once again. You can't take her away too soon from Ezra. He needs her."

"I know. I am worried about him. He was happy to see her and didn't hesitate for a minute to hug her. I couldn't do that. I can't forgive her."

"It's funny how children can forgive and forget so easily while adults hold onto grudges and cannot forgive as easily."

"I guess that's true, Branyrd. But what can I do? I found someone else I want to spend the rest of my life with – Amy, and Ezra loves her too."

"Lucas, I'm sorry I took so long to get here. There were some issues I had to take care of but now I'm here. Was Ezra surprised? I wish I could have seen his face," Amy stopped talking when she saw the stricken look on Lucas's face. She almost dropped the present she had for Ezra.

"Amy, I…I…almost forgot you were coming. Thank you. Ezra will be happy to see you and open a new present." Lucas tried to wipe away the tears that threatened to fall on his sleeve by turning away quickly.

Branyrd rescued him by taking Amy in to see Ezra. "Let me take you to the birthday boy so he can open your present. He will be thrilled to open another one. He was quite excited and surprised to say the least."

Lucas followed close behind ready to make the dreaded introductions of his wife to his girlfriend.

Once Ezra spotted Amy and his present he jumped up and took it from Amy's hands and put it on the table so he could hug her. "Thank you so much, Amy, for coming to my party. You missed the surprise. I was so happy that I jumped up and down!" Ezra giggled. "What did you get me?"

"I wouldn't have missed your party for the world, Ezra. You are one special little boy to me. I love you bunches."

"I love you bunches too, Amy! My mommy came too."

"What?" Amy asked in shock as a woman came to stand next to her.

"Hi, I'm Ezra's mother. Who are you?" Kylie looked Amy up and down appraising her as Amy did the same thing to Kylie.

Both women stood there staring at one another until Lucas came beside them to make the introductions.

"Lucas, I don't understand. I thought..." Amy began but turned and walked away before she said anything more.

"Amy, wait a minute. Let me explain," Lucas cried out as he ran after her.

Kylie watched the duo in alarm. She sat next to her son while he opened his latest present.

"Mommy, where is Amy going? She didn't wait until I opened my present."

"I don't know, sweetie. What is it?"

"Oh, my goodness! It's a superman costume with a mask, cape and everything. I love it! Look, here is a DVD with Superman on it. Can I watch it now?"

"Maybe a little later, Ezra. Right now, I must speak to your daddy."

Kylie walked over to where Amy and Lucas were in deep conversation. She cleared her throat and asked, "Is this your girlfriend, Lucas?"

"It's not your concern, Kylie. You left us long ago. We are no longer married as far as I am concerned. I want a divorce to make it legal."

"A divorce? What are you talking about? I came back to begin anew. I needed to see my son. I'm sorry if you can't understand what I have been going through. Won't you even listen to me?"

"No, I don't want to listen to you, Kylie. I suggest you get yourself a lawyer and so will I."

Amy pulled away from Lucas but he held firmly to her hand. "Don't leave, Amy. You belong here, she doesn't," he said as he gave his estranged wife a look of anger and disappointment.

"All right. If that is what you want, Lucas. I need to say goodbye to my son first. I will have to explain to Ezra why you are making me leave."

"Wait, Kylie. I will tell him. Say your goodbyes and don't call me unless you agree to a divorce. I will have my lawyer get in touch with yours. That way I won't have to talk to you any more afterward."

"What about visitation rights with Ezra? I need to see him, Lucas."

"Why? You left him two years ago and never wanted visitation rights all that time."

"I know, I'm sorry. I couldn't deal with anything then."

"What makes you think you can deal with anything now, Kylie? You don't appear to be free and clear of whatever drugs or alcohol you were taking. I can't have my son near you in your state."

"I am trying, Lucas. It is difficult, but I am trying."

"Well, you better try harder or you will never see my son again."

"He's our son, Lucas."

"As far as I am concerned, he is my son and my son alone. You gave up all rights to him a long time ago."

Kylie went back to see Ezra and give him a last hug before leaving. "Sorry, I have to go now, Ezra. I will see you again soon."

"But, Mommy, where are you going? You just got here."

"I have something I have to do, Ezra. Be a good boy and I will see you again soon. I promise." Ezra's eyes opened wider as he watched his mother's face droop and look sad.

"Are you sad, Mommy? Because I will be sad if you leave. I know you won't be back like before when you left me with the lady. You never came back," Ezra began to cry.

"Oh, Ezra. I am sick. I am so sorry. I could not take care of you back then and I don't think I can take care of you now. I am still not well. Please forgive me, sweetie. I love you and always will."

"I love you too, Mommy, but I don't know why you have to leave."

"Daddy will explain it all to you. Take care and be a good boy for your father, Ezra."

"Mommy! Don't leave!" Ezra ran after her and grabbed her hand to try to stop her.

Lucas came forward and held Ezra back, releasing his wife's hand so she could leave. Kylie sniffled but never looked back.

"Why is she leaving me again, Daddy? I don't like her. I'm mad at her."

"I know, little man. I understand. I am mad at her too. But we will talk about it more later. Why don't we go over and play with your new train set. I haven't seen the racing cars yet. Let's race them."

"Yeah, Daddy, let's race them. I bet I can beat you!" Ezra went back to the trains and sat down to find the racing cars, wiping his tears away.

Amy was still standing there in shock. Branyrd took her aside and offered her a cup of coffee. "Come sit down, Amy. Lucas needs to talk to you. Give him some time to spend with Ezra first. He loves you, you know. Give him some space to get his life in order."

"I don't know what to make of her coming here. Why did she come now after all this time?"

"I don't know. I guess she remembered it was Ezra's birthday today. She saw Lucas's photo in the newspaper in an article about this place."

"Oh, but why did she wait all this time and never call him to find out how Ezra was doing? What kind of mother would do that?"

"I don't know, Amy. Only she can answer that question. You and Lucas may never get the answer. I wish I could help. Stay close to him. He needs you to help him get through this with Kylie."

"I plan to keep close. I love Lucas like I never loved anyone in my life and Ezra is so precious to me. I feel as if he is my own son," Amy responded in a choked voice.

***

Lucas played with Ezra for another half hour and then excused himself to see Amy. He had kept watch over her and Branyrd as they were talking and having their coffee. He was concerned she would leave him too now. He couldn't lose her.

He would make a call to Sanora later today to begin proceedings for a divorce that will give him a chance for a new beginning.

CHAPTER THIRTY-SIX

Kylie sat in her car and cried until she couldn't cry anymore. What was she to do now? Lucas would never forgive her and take her back. He loved another.

She called her lawyer and asked to meet. She had to figure out a way to stay in her son's life no matter what. As she drove away she looked one more time at the building and saw her son through the large window talking to his father. Lucas looked up at that moment and met Kylie's eyes as she dropped her head and drove away.

Lucas turned to his son. "Ezra, I need to talk to Amy. Can you play with your trains again? I will be back to play with you soon."

"Okay, Daddy. Tell Amy she can come play with me too. Tell her I love the present she gave me. Superman is my favorite superhero!"

"I will, Ezra. I'm sure she will be happy to hear that and want to check out your awesome train set."

"Okay. See you later, Daddy."

Amy watched Lucas as he came forward and sat down next to her. Branyrd excused herself and left them alone.

"I'm so sorry, Amy. I had no idea Kylie was coming. I told her I want a divorce and she will need to get a lawyer and that she is not welcome here."

"I heard you say that, Lucas. I was right next to you when you grabbed my arm and wouldn't let me get away. It was quite uncomfortable to witness it."

"I can imagine. But I wanted you to know that I did not want her in my life because I love you. I did not want to lose you because she was back."

"What are you saying, Lucas?" Amy asked, her stomach doing somersaults.

"I didn't want to do this now. I had planned to take you out to dinner and do it right but, Amy, will you marry me?" Lucas got down on his knee.

"Oh, Lucas, I...I..." Amy stuttered in disbelief.

"I don't have the ring yet but I will get it. Will you marry me, Amy?" Lucas's eyes showed his anxiety and desperation.

"I…I… Yes, I will, Lucas. I love you too. I can't imagine life without you and Ezra."

"Oh, Amy! I love you so much! I promise I will get you a ring, a beautiful one. In fact, you can help me pick it out tomorrow. Okay?"

"You don't have to do that so soon. It's okay, Lucas. I know we are not officially engaged yet until I have a ring but I feel like I am your fiancé just the same."

"You have made me the luckiest guy in the world. I can't…I…"

Amy put her arms out to Lucas and enfolded him in her embrace as they both shed tears of joy and relief.

Branyrd watched this display as did others and a clapping sound broke out that reverberated around the room causing Amy and Lucas to look back at the group and laugh.

"Congratulations, you two!" Branyrd said as she came closer.

"Thank you, Branyrd. We are not quite officially engaged until I get the ring but plan to do that tomorrow."

"Good to know, Lucas. I am happy for you both and wish you good health and all the happiness that is coming to you both and Ezra."

"Thank you. All I need now is to get the divorce. I guess I need to get a lawyer."

"I think I know one that would be perfect for you," Branyrd winked and smirked at the couple.

"I think I know who you mean, Branyrd. That is who I planned to call soon."

"She is coming over today to finalize the paperwork for Nick's office. I'll have her come see you."

"Great. Thanks again, Branyrd. That will save me a call." Lucas smiled and sighed happily as he squeezed Amy's hand in his.

CHAPTER THIRTY-SEVEN

Later that day Sanora stopped by to see Branyrd and have her and Nick sign the paperwork. Before she left, Branyrd told her to see Lucas.

"Is everything all right?" Sanora asked in confusion.

"I'll let him tell you." Branyrd called out to Lucas who was putting all Ezra's presents together to bring to their new home. "Sanora is here."

"Hi Sanora. Sorry to bother you. I should have called for an appointment but Branyrd told me you were going to be here anyway."

"Yes, that's okay. What can I do for you, Lucas?"

"I want to hire you to start divorce proceedings for me and my estranged wife. I hope there won't be any problems from her. She may try to get visitation rights with Ezra."

"Okay. We need to meet in my office. Call my secretary and set up an appointment. Bring any correspondence and proof of your marriage at that time."

"That will be easy. All I have is the marriage license. There has been no correspondence from her until today. She left us two years ago."

"She never called to check up on Ezra?" Sanora asked in surprise.

"No, never. I didn't even know where she had gone."

"I don't think you will have any problems, Lucas. She abandoned both you and her son. Let's talk more in my office."

"Thank you, Sanora. I'll call your office shortly."

Lucas let out a sigh of relief and smiled at Amy who was still by his side holding onto his hand.

"Do you want me to go with you, Lucas?" Amy asked.

"I don't think so. But I will keep you in the loop, don't worry."

"Okay, Lucas. You know where to find me."

"I do you. You will be at my apartment with me."

"What? You want me to move in with you. You just got the apartment and still not settled yet. That was generous of the bank to give you a loan. But, after all, you do have all these buildings now as collateral."

"Yes, I do! I keep forgetting that. I needed to get a loan to get started furnishing our apartment, buy a car and whatever else we need now that we are not going to be homeless. The bank manager was quite complimentary about the work we have done here and how it has changed the city for the better. I don't want him to be sorry he approved a loan, so I plan to get another job working with Nick in addition to your store in order to make my payments. So, what do you say, Amy? Is this arrangement okay with you? You can bring your stuff over and we will get settled together. Sound good?"

"Sounds great. I will have to cancel my lease on my apartment and move all my stuff to yours. Can you help me or do I need to get a moving van? At least let me bring all my furniture since you don't have any yet. Right?" Better yet, you can come live with me. It would be a lot easier, wouldn't it?

"Well, I don't know. We can discuss this further. How much do you have to move, Amy?" Lucas almost choked on his words.

"Not too much, but enough to furnish your apartment so you will not have to buy anything. Come over tonight for dinner and we can decide together."

"Sounds good, Amy. Thank you, but I don't want to take advantage of your generosity. I do have the loan to take care of all this."

"You won't be taking advantage of me, Lucas. We are going to be a family, after all. Remember? Besides, you will need the money to buy a car and other stuff you will need."

"Yes, you are right, Amy. Okay, Ezra and I will be over."

Lucas smiled and felt happy for once in his life. He knew this was only the beginning of a whole new life for him, Ezra and Amy.

***

Branyrd summoned Benedicto, "I need you, Guardian Angel. Where are you?"

Benedicto appeared behind Branyrd and she nearly jumped out of her human skin. "Why do you do that, Benedicto?"

"Sorry, little Angel. Didn't mean to frighten you. Did you realize you didn't jump but elevated a few feet off the ground?"

"I did? I didn't even notice I did that. Does that mean I can fly?"

"Well, one way to find out. Try flying up now with me."

Benedicto flew up into the dark sky and looked down on Branyrd who rocked back and forth lifting one leg then the other.

"What's wrong, little Angel? Try lifting both feet at the same time."

"Oh, I can't seem to do that. Wait, I did it! I'm flying, Benedicto, just like you! I can't believe it! Look at me!"

"Yes, Branyrd, you are flying. Now try to steer to the right and then the left. There you go. You've got it now. So proud of you, little Angel!"

"Thank you, Benedicto. Do you think it is time to leave now? Everything is set in motion with Lucas and Ezra; Nick is now the owner of his place, and all paperwork is in order for the whole complex and under Lucas's name. What else do I need to do?"

"I don't know, Branyrd, maybe you should ask HIM if you are all done with this mission."

Branyrd raised her head and looked skyward. "LORD, am I done here?"

"You have done a marvelous job, Branyrd. I can't praise you enough. I am pleased with your work. You will be leaving in the morning with enough time to say your goodbyes."

"Tomorrow morning? I'm leaving tomorrow morning? Oh….my goodness. So soon, LORD."

"I have given you more than enough time, Branyrd, and you have fulfilled your obligations here with all these people. You have given them a new lease on life and a purpose."

"They do seem happier than before. I'm relieved I could do something worthwhile to assist them."

"See you soon, Angel." A titter could be heard that dissipated and then disappeared as if it never existed.

"Benedicto, what am I to do? I have to say goodbye to everyone."

"Yes, you do. It's time, little Angel."

"Okay. I hope the morning doesn't come too soon. I will miss everyone."

Benedicto had flown upward and disappeared when she looked around for him.

That figures, he always disappears when I am talking. I guess he has had enough of me. Branyrd sighed and smiled to herself feeling full and happy all went so well on her second mission.

***

Branyrd's cell rang in her pocket. She had forgotten she still had it. She planned to give it to Lucas. She answered the call. "Hello."

"Hi Branyrd. I told you I would call back to let you know if I got a new job. Well, guess where I am?"

"Where, Alice?" Branyrd smiled trying to picture where Alice was now.

"I am now the secretary to the governor of this marvelous state of New Hampshire! How do you like that?"

"Wow! That is fantastic, Alice! I met the governor. He is a lovely man. You are fortunate to work for him."

"I know, right? Also, something good happened. The mayor is in jail for his errant ways with the drug cartel, etc. Isn't that great to hear?"

"My goodness, yes, that is good news. I guess he will have to atone for what he did. I am so happy for you, Alice."

"Thank you, Branyrd. I will stop by soon to see you at the opening of the site."

"I…I…won't be there, Alice. Sorry. I must leave to go on another mission elsewhere. But I want you to know I am honored to have met you and that we were friends. I appreciate your support of all of us here at the community."

"Oh, no, Branyrd. You can't leave now. All this would have not been possible without you," Alice said with a shocked voice choked with sadness.

"Well, thank you, Alice. But I was only the helper in all this. All things were possible without me. I was only along for the ride to help the music play."

"Music?" Alice asked in confusion.

"Oh, that's just a metaphor. Sorry, Alice. Take care and enjoy your new job and say hello to Governor Crosley for me."

"Thank you, Branyrd, I will. Take care wherever you go. It was my pleasure to know and love you."

"Love you too, Alice. Goodbye."

"Bye for now, Branyrd. I will see you again one day, I am sure."

***

Time inevitably came for Branyrd to make the rounds to all the beds to say her goodbyes. Fred, Gloria and Harold hugged her and didn't want to let go.

"Hey, don't worry. I will be watching over you all."

"Does that mean we have to behave ourselves?" Harold said with a guffaw.

"I don't know about you, Harold. You don't know how to behave yourself," Branyrd giggled and gave him another hug.

"Stay safe and well, Harold. I will miss you."

"Missing you already, little lady," he said with a tear in his eye.

"None of that, Harold. I don't want to cry too because I may not stop."

Fred whispered to Branyrd, "I think I will be seeing you soon. HE came to me last night and said I will be going to see my wife."

"What did you say, Fred?" Branyrd asked in disbelief.

"I am going to the hereafter, little one. It's time and I'm ready."

"Oh, Fred. You will love it there. I will miss you most of all. You are one sweet man. Say hello to your wife."

"I will, Angel. I will."

Branyrd stopped and looked at Fred. "What did you call me, Fred?"

"Huh? I didn't say anything."

"Hmm. Okay."

Gloria was next to stop Branyrd in her tracks when she announced, "I am going to be leaving soon too, Branyrd. I'm ready to go. I am so tired but wanted to stay here long enough to see this through. It is all so beautiful, thanks to you, Branyrd. You did this for all of us. Thank you so much."

Gloria's eyes filled and tears ran down making tracks in her wrinkles.

"Where are you going, Gloria?" Branyrd asked, afraid to hear the answer that she suspected for a long time.

"I am ready to meet my maker. You know HIM, don't you, Branyrd?"

"What? You are much better, Gloria. You aren't sick anymore."

"But I am, Branyrd. I just hide it well. Maybe I will see you again sometime," Gloria hugged Branyrd, smiled and winked as she went back to her bed to lay down.

Branyrd tried not to show her heartache and the tears that kept coming. She closed her eyes and whispered to HIM, "Are you taking both of them, LORD?"

HE whispered back, "It is time for them, Branyrd. Don't worry, Angel. I will be taking good care of them."

"I know YOU will, LORD. I am just sad to see them leave. What about Ezra? He will be devastated to lose them both, his adopted grandparents."

"Don't worry about Ezra. I will take care of him and keep him busy. I will let you see them all one more time as I did before, Angel. Okay?"

"Yes, I want to see them all again. I will miss them terribly," Branyrd sighed and sniffled.

The Angel went to visit Nick and the other Marines who were in his new office. "You are extraordinary and talented young men. I can't thank you enough for all you have done here to make this all possible. I am saddened I must leave you but it is time for me to move on to help others in need."

"We will miss you, Branyrd. We owe you so much for giving us our lives back with a purpose. We are going to be so busy there won't be time to get bored anymore. Right, guys?" Nick exclaimed.

A round of agreements could be heard as each man came over to hug Branyrd and say a few words of thanks. The Angel at this point was openly crying.

"Sorry about my blubbering. I will miss you all so much. Keep up the good work, men. I will be watching you."

Lucas came into the office and took Branyrd aside. "Are you really leaving us now, Branyrd? I heard everyone say you were."

"Yes, unfortunately, it is time for me, Lucas. Good luck to you, Amy and Ezra I wish you much happiness in your future together. Don't worry too much about Kylie, she will come around and accept what has to be. Do let her see Ezra from time to time. She will need him as much as he will need her."

"I will to a limit, Branyrd. I will do my best."

"Oh, before I forget, here is my phone. I won't need it where I am going. Also, don't forget the bank account is in your name if you need any money to keep this place going. Here is the paperwork for it and this place. There is plenty in the account thanks to Alice's efforts and those of so many others in the community."

"Thank you, Branyrd. That's good to know. I'm sure we will be needing more to keep the supplies well stocked and for any other items or problems that could come up."

"You are welcome. You are an exceptional person, Lucas. I am honored to have known you and spent time with you and your precious son. I will miss you both so much." Branyrd wiped her tears that kept flowing and blew her nose when given a tissue by Lucas.

"Same here, Branyrd. You have changed my life for the better. I can't say thank you enough. I hope one day you will come back to see us."

"I…I don't know, Lucas. But I will keep an eye on you. Work hard and have a good life. This community is now fully in your hands. Watch over them all to ensure it stays this way."

"I promise to do that, Branyrd. I will make sure that they are kept busy to help keep it this way. Each person will have a job to do to keep the facilities running smoothly. I think Harold will make sure that everyone pulls his weight. Some of them are already planning to set up a little store and sell things that they make like crocheted, knitted items and cookies. Don't worry about anything, Branyrd. Take care and be well, my wonder of a woman."

Branyrd hugged Lucas again and smiled. "I can see that you have everything in control. Oh, I am not a wonder of a woman but that is kind of you to say. Goodbye, Lucas."

Ezra was standing behind Branyrd and she nearly knocked him over when she turned around. "Oh, sorry, little guy. I didn't see you."

"Were you going to leave without saying goodbye to me too, Aunt Branyrd?" Ezra asked with tears in his eyes.

"No, of course not, Ezra. You are my favorite little guy in this whole wide world and beyond. You take care of your daddy and Amy for me. I must leave but I will keep an eye on you. Have fun in school and work hard."

"I will. I can't wait to start. Daddy already bought me clothes and new sneakers to wear. We visited my school and I got to see my classroom. It is really big and has so many desks. I think I know which one I want to sit at. Daddy even said if I am good, he will get me a puppy!"

"A puppy, how exciting! Wow, that's terrific to hear, Ezra! See you later, alligator."

"In a while, crocodile! Aunt Branyrd? I love you!" Ezra responded as a lone tear trailed across his cheek. He gave Branyrd one more tight hug before turning to go to Amy who hugged him as he openly cried.

"I love you too, Ezra. Please don't cry. I will be watching over you."

Lucas walked Branyrd outside with his arm around her shoulder and looked around. Where is your car. Who is picking you up?"

Benedicto appeared behind Lucas and tapped him on the shoulder. "Here I am. I am her transportation even though she can now do it on her own."

"What?" Lucas asked in confusion.

"No worries, Lucas. I am all set. Benedicto will escort me on my way. Goodbye, my friend."

Lucas hugged Branyrd tightly one more time, shook Benedicto's large hand and then turned back to the office to talk to Nick, heard a whoosh and looked around. Branyrd and Benedicto were nowhere in sight.

"I wonder. Is she really an Angel...? No, it can't be," he shook his head and looked around again with a sigh.

EPILOGUE

Branyrd looked through the window the LORD provided for her last glimpse of Earth and the community she had helped.

She smiled as they had the official opening of the site as Lucas, Nick, Doc and the other Marines and helpers were presented with a plaque by Governor Crosley that would be placed at City Hall for all to see of their efforts to make the community a better place for all.

Branyrd looked up at the sign outside the community and gasped in surprise – it read 'Branyrd's Community Center.'

She watched as Ezra held up the plaque with his father's help wearing a brilliant smile as they both held onto Amy's hands, her left hand now sported a shiny diamond. They were a family in a sense, even if not married yet.

Branyrd was now in her Angel's body and couldn't shed tears as before but still she felt a feeling of joy as her wings sparkled and fluttered around her causing a brilliant rainbow to appear above the heads of the people who were celebrating the opening of the center.

Lucas looked up and smiled.

ABOUT THE AUTHOR

Janice Spina is a retired administrative secretary from a public school system in Massachusetts. She has always loved writing poetry, novels, and children's stories. She published her first book in 2013 and has not stopped since.

This is the 42nd book Janice has published. She also has two mystery series of six books each, one for boys and the other for girls even though they are enjoyed by both boys and girls. She has a fantasy series of two books with more to come for YA.

Janice has published 20 children's stories for young children. She also writes under J.E. Spina and has published six novels and a short story collection for 18+.

She can be reached at these links.

Website: http://Jemsbooks.com
Blog: https://Jemsbooks.blog
Twitter: http://twitter.com/janice_spina
FB Main Page: http://facebook.com/janice.spina.9
FB Author Page: http://facebook.com/janicespina7
FB Novelist Page: http://facebook.com/jespina7

Janice lives in New Hampshire with her husband, John, and two tanks of fish. John is the illustrator of her children's books and designer of all her book covers.

If you enjoyed this book, please leave a review where you purchased it and spread the word to your family and friends. Janice loves to hear from readers and welcomes reviews from wherever her books are purchased. She says, 'It's like Christmas each time I receive a review!'

If you would like to be on Janice Spina's email list to receive updates, newsletters, and special deals on books, please follow her at her blog/website above.

Watch for more books coming from Jemsbooks.

A NOTE FROM THE AUTHOR

This is the second book in this series about an angel. I infused some comedy into this sometimes-serious story. It deals with many issues that are evident in our world today. I hope you will find it entertaining.

This series is written for young adults – Ages 17+ but younger teens may find it entertaining too. I hope you enjoyed this work of fiction. Watch for more books in this series coming over the new few years.

Thank you for purchasing one of Jemsbooks. I appreciate your kind support of me and my books. If you like this book, a review would be greatly appreciated wherever you purchased it. Reviews and word of mouth are the best way to spread your thoughts about books. Please share your review with friends and family. I would love to hear from you. You can reach me at jjspina(@comcast.net.

All my books are available on Amazon and Barnes & Noble. Watch for more books coming for all ages.

With Blessings & Love,

Janice Spina

OTHER MG/PT/YA BOOKS BY JANICE SPINA for 10+

Davey & Derek Junior Detectives Book 1: The Case of the Missing Cell Phone
Pinnacle Book Achievement Award, Honorable Mention- Readers' Favorite Book Award

Davey & Derek Junior Detectives Book 2: The Case of the Mysterious Black Cat
Pinnacle Book Achievement Award

Davey & Derek Junior Detectives Book 3: The Case of the Magical Ivory Elephant
Pinnacle Book Achievement Award
Reader's Favorite Book Awards – Silver Medal

Davey & Derek Junior Detectives Book 4: The Case of the Brown Scraggly Dog
Top Shelf Book Awards – First Place
Finalist in Red City Review Awards
5-Star Book Review – Readers' Favorite Book Awards

Davey & Derek Junior Detectives Book 5: The Case of the Sad Mischievous Ghost
Pinnacle Book Achievement Award & Authorsdb
Cover Contest – Silver Medal

Davey & Derek Junior Detectives Book 6: The Case of the Mystery of the Bells
Pinnacle Book Achievement Award
Finalist – Readers' Favorite Book Awards
Finalist – Book Excellence Awards

Abby & Holly School Dance
Pinnacle Book Achievement Award
Bronze Medal from Readers' Favorite Book Awards

Abby & Holly Series Book 2: Unfortunate Events
Pinnacle Book Achievement Award
Readers' Favorite Book Awards – Honorable Mention

Abby & Holly Series, Book 3, Secrets of the Trunk
Pinnacle Book Achievement Award

Abby & Holly Series, Book 4, The Hidden Stairway

Pinnacle Book Achievement Award

Abby & Holly Series, Book 5, The Copper Key

Pinnacle Book Achievement Award

Abby & Holly Series, Book 6, Faulty Timeline

Pinnacle Book Achievement Award

YA BOOKS BY JANICE SPINA for 15+

The Legend of the Taken Ones (Gateskin Chronicles Book 1)

5-Star Review from Readers' Favorite Book Awards

Finalist - Book Excellence Awards

The Unknown Territory (Gateskin Chronicles Book 2)

BOOKS BY J.E. SPINA FOR 18+

Hunting Mariah

   (Finalist in Authorsdb First Lines Contest)

Mariah's Revenge

   (Finalist in Authorsdb First Lines Contest)

How Far is Heaven

An Angel Among Us: A Short Story Collection

In A Second

Lubelia Alycea: One Hundred Years

The Misunderstood Angel: Branyrd the Angel Series Book 1

www.ingramcontent.com/pod-product-compliance
Lightning Source LLC
Chambersburg PA
CBHW051246260626
47162CB00002B/640